The (Revised) Protocols of the Elders of Zion

Stories of Neurotic Obsession

For Howard, Mel, Larry, Lenny, Sarah, Gary, Lewis, Gilbert, Al and all the wacky, misunderstood Elders.

Table of Contents

Yellow Cab Blues

Needleman knew it was going to be a bad day right from the get-go. Because of the rain, it took him nearly 15 minutes to find a cab and when he finally got one, it was that damned Paul Sorvino pretentiously telling him to fasten his seatbelt. "Actor, singer, chef, New Yorker, seatbelt wearer." Needleman far preferred Joe Torre's, "Don't forget to take your receipt and personal belongings. I'll see you at the stadium." If they insisted on having those stupid greetings, his simple message was ideal and Torre was the right man to deliver it. Needleman believed it was Torre who'd said that pizza was like sex: Even when it was bad it was still pretty good.

*

With a start, Needleman realized the cabbie had made a wrong turn. Instead of continuing south on Broadway, he'd turned left on 66th Street, apparently planning to go through Central Park—a common error going crosstown. The absence of traffic lights on the transverse road was enticing, but whatever time one saved was more than offset by Queensboro Bridge congestion on the other side. Broadway was the way to go— Broadway down to 57th Street, across to Lexington, then down again to 48th and Bear International's Worldwide Headquarters. On average, Broadway took two minutes less than the park. This didn't sound like much, but on a 20-minute trip represented an efficiency gain of ten percent.

Needleman could tell you the best route between any two points in the city. It was his thing—like that guy who could multiply six-digit numbers in his head. But he said nothing. The cabbie didn't tell Needleman how to be a stockbroker and Needleman wasn't about to tell him how to drive his cab. It was an unspoken expression of mutual respect between two men. Needleman sat back and waited patiently.

The rain was coming down pretty good, and when they got to Madison and 48th, where the cabbie needed to make a left, the intersection was flooded. He continued down to 46th Street, which was flooded too.

"We go west to get around," the driver said without taking his eyes off the road. He turned right on 45th Street, presumably intending to turn back on Park Avenue and make another attempt at approaching the East Side from an uptown street. Traffic was heavy on Park, though, and after an abortive effort to force the cab into the flow of traffic, the driver continued west on 45th, past Sixth Avenue, which was as bad as Park, past Seventh and Broadway, which went downtown, and past Eighth, which wasn't quite as bad as the others, but still pretty bad.

"We take shortcut," the driver said. "Save time."

He continued driving west—straight into the Lincoln Tunnel and Hoboken, New Jersey.

*

As the cab neared the Delaware Water Gap, Needleman checked the license, which was encased in plastic and mounted on the partition. The driver's name was Vijay Singh. Needleman wondered whether this caused him any grief, as Vijay Singh was also the name of a prominent professional golfer. Needleman imagined the sort of things people might say.

"So, the golf thing didn't pan out, eh?"

"Been to Fiji recently?" (Vijay the Golfer was from Fiji.)

"Take me to Augusta and step on it."

It must have made Vijay angry enough to slam the brakes and propel passengers into the partition. Despite Sorvino and Torre's warnings, hardly anybody wore their seat belts in cabs. Naso-cranial fractures were the seventh most common injury in city hospitals.

Needleman didn't much like his own name either. More accurately, he didn't like being called Needleman. His given name was Ethan, which was fine, but everyone at work called him Needleman. His fate had been sealed his first day on the job when Lucas Flounder, the head of personal investment management, summoned Needleman to his cubicle.

"What do you like to be called?" Flounder asked.

"Ethan is fine," said Needleman.

"All right, Needleman, get to work," Flounder said.

From that day forward Needleman was Needleman. He sometimes considered protesting, but after 17 years you just don't walk into the Bear one day, wolf down a bacon sandwich, and declare that you henceforth want to be known by a new name. After 17 years, even Needleman thought of himself as Needleman.

Flounder was a real prick. He fancied himself to be a Big Swinging Dick like the bond traders in *Liar's Poker*. Truth was Flounder only had his job because his father hosted *The Flounder Report*, a popular CNN financial show. Flounder only wished he could be like the heroes of Michael Lewis's book. Those guys were trailblazers; Flounder was just a salesman. True, he was Needleman's boss, but that would someday change. Needleman had been plotting Flounder's undoing for more than a decade. No progress had yet been made, but Needleman felt confident that uppances would be coming soon.

*

Somewhere around Pittsburgh, it became apparent that Vijay Singh was planning to drive around the earth and approach Lexington Avenue from the east. This wasn't the ideal route. Needleman performed a quick calculation and determined that it would take approximately 23 days to circumnavigate the globe, not including time to cross the Atlantic and Pacific Oceans.

Even allowing for bad weather, this represented a substantial efficiency loss.

Moreover, the crosstown fare, which was usually either $8.30 or $8.60 depending on lights, would be approximately 10,000 times greater. Part of this was due to the extra 24,900 miles they'd need to drive, but the big hit was that cab rates doubled outside the city. Moreover, Needleman's calculation excluded tolls. He had no idea how much it cost to cross bridges and tunnels in other parts of the world. He'd been to England once, but that was before they'd built the Chunnel, and you couldn't drive through the Chunnel anyway.

Needleman didn't like the uncertainty. He considered telling the cabbie to turn around, but dismissed the idea. The whole thing was on him, really. If he'd been against going west, he should have said so in the first place.

*

Between Des Moines and Omaha, Needleman realized that he needed the bathroom. It wasn't yet a full-blown emergency, but would be soon enough. Needleman thanked his lucky stars that he always drank his three cups of coffee at the office, where it was provided free, rather than his apartment. Coffee ran through him like shit through a goose. Even without the coffee, though, he wouldn't be able to hold it forever.

Needleman considered, but rejected, asking the cabdriver to pull over. In addition to the four dollars per mile for travel outside the city, cabs charged 40 cents for every minute of waiting time. No way would Needleman pay two bucks to go to the bathroom. He'd wait until Vijay needed the head. If Vijay initiated the stop, he'd have to pause the meter. Then Needleman could go for free. Needleman reclined and tried to think about something other than his bladder.

*

To pass time, Needleman began attacking a sesame seed, which he believed was lodged between the second upper cuspid and first bicuspid on the right side of his mouth.

He began half-heartedly, but soon was attacking with fervor, arching his tongue backward and then flicking downward against the bilingual pits behind his teeth to generate the maximum possible force. This seed was a tough customer.

The Day of Embedding was Super Bowl Sunday 1985. Louis Scuteri, one of the Big Swinging Dicks in mortgage-backed securities hosted a pre-game brunch. Scuteri, like Flounder, was a diehard Cowboys fan. Everyone understood that there would be no rooting for the Broncos. Even passive rooting was disdained. All the junior traders, Needleman included, feared that Scuteri would sense any negative energy. If the Cowboys lost, the consequences at work on Monday would be devastating.

Needleman hated the Cowboys. Everything from Tom Landry's hat to Danny White's insistence on quarterbacking and punting to the fans' smug confidence in victory oozed pretension. Needleman preferred the Bills. He believed losing built character.

To make matters worse, Scuteri's spread contained only sesame bagels.

"Everyone loves sesame," Scuteri said.

Needleman hated sesame. Diverticulitis ran in his family. But it was sesame or nothing that day and Needleman didn't want to make waves so he ate one. A decade and a half later, he was still living with the consequences.

The resilience of the seed caused an existential quandary. Fourteen years is a long time to flick anything, and

Needleman's efforts had borne no fruit. Sometimes he doubted himself.

What if the seed weren't actually there? What if he'd been probing for nothing? That would mean he'd invested thousands of hours in trying to fix something that had never been broken or, more accurately, had never existed. If he could buy into a fiction, then how could he trust his other foundational beliefs like the importance of dental floss and carpeting?

Needleman told himself that the problem was, between work and trips to the allergist, he didn't have the time to attack the seed properly. Now he had nothing but time.

*

In Spokane, Washington, Vijay Singh turned north and headed for the Seward Peninsula. As recently as five million years ago (or as long as 7.3 million years, depending on an ongoing debate centered on the Astarte mollusk), Asia was linked to North America by a thin land bridge across what is now known as the Bering Strait. Though the bridge had long since disappeared, it was the point where Eurasia and North America came closest to meeting. From Alaska, they'd have to cross merely 100 miles of water to reach Russia.

As the cab wound its way up a narrow two-lane highway through the Coast Mountains of Vancouver, Needleman grew increasingly aware of his need to pee. Though Vijay had been driving for three days straight, he showed no signs of slowing. At one point, Needleman peeked into the driver's cabin to see whether Vijay had made any special accommodations for himself. Needleman saw neither catheters nor colostomy bags, but Vijay's bladder was distended to watermelon size. Needleman had read about this adaptation among truck drivers, some of whom could go for weeks without urinating. The world record was eleven months, held by Heinrich Schlictman of Stuttgart, a former tightrope walker who lost his nerve and thereafter dedicated himself to increasing his bladder capacity by consuming large quantities of a sickening (and highly acidic) mixture of lime and grapefruit juice. He competed in the world bladder control championships, held in Munich during Oktoberfest. It wasn't as exciting or as lucrative as competitive hot dog eating, but Schlictman had made name for himself.

Vijay Singh might not be in Heinrich Schlictman's league, but he was close. Needleman felt envious. Unless they stopped at a bathroom soon, he was going to die of nitrogen narcosis.

*

The ferry from Wales, Alaska to Naukan, Russia runs only once a day, but by chance the cab arrived just as the barge's doors were closing, depriving Needleman of an opportunity to relieve himself at a Port-O-San behind the stationhouse. Once aboard, they were sealed inside the cab. The belly of the ferry accommodated three rows of two cars, which were spaced no more than an inch from each other and the surrounding walls, making it impossible to open a door. An attendant walked along the hoods to collect the fare (the equivalent of $59). As he took the money, he said something to Vijay in a foreign language, presumably Russian. Vijay responded in the same tongue, rolled down the window, and slid through a paper—apparently a visa, which the attendant examined and returned before moving on to the next hood.

Who was Vijay Singh? He'd driven from Manhattan to Alaska without once consulting a map. He'd navigated downtown Saskatoon like an old pro. Now it appeared he was also a polyglot. Needleman had so many questions. Where was he from? Why did he carry a visa? And, most importantly: Did he ever pee?

*

Needleman had envisioned Siberia as an earthly hell— home to Solzhenitsyn's gulags and fat, ugly, tractor-driving women betrothed to exiled ex-convicts. Instead he found a land of endless forest—the great Russian Taiga, which stretches from the Sea of Japan to the Gulf of Finland. Periodically, they'd pass through a quaint wooden village where they'd see the occasional wedding party and a surprising number of ice cream stands. In Ulan Ude, they passed the world's largest bust of Lenin. There, their progress was momentarily slowed by a horse-driven milk truck, which blocked the one-lane road, leading Vijay to honk maniacally. Needleman feared this would create an international incident, but the milkman handled the situation with equanimity, pulled to the side and waved the cab by.

Near Krasnayarsk, the Siberian capital, Needleman finally surrendered and asked Vijay to stop. Without a word, Vijay pulled onto the shoulder. Needleman expected Singh to get out, at which point Needleman planned to demand that they share the waiting-time charges, but Singh didn't move. He mindlessly extracted some earwax and watched the meter.

Ordinarily this would have angered Needleman, but he felt a sense of calm. Truth was, he'd always wanted to see this part of Russia. In 1908, a cosmic object landed mysteriously in the Siberian wilderness. The explosion created a distinctive pattern of tree fall around the Podkamennaza Tunguska River, but no discernable crater. Some suspected it might an alien landing site.

As Needleman peed, he took it all in—or rather the ground immediately in front of him. He preferred to urinate in a typewriter-like pattern, proceeding left to right until he reached the limit of his range when he'd return to the left, slightly lower. About halfway down the right-hand side of his page, Needleman noticed a round piece of manufactured metal, about an inch in diameter. Maybe, just maybe, he thought, it was from Outer Space.

Needleman was so excited by the prospect that he lost track of time. His plan had been to evacuate in less than 60 seconds, but ultimately took three minutes, which would cost him $1.20. Even this didn't sour his mood. Back in the cab, he reclined and carefully examined the metallic sphere, which he ultimately determined to be a Tapxyh Tarragon Soda bottle cap.

This only modestly dampened the thrill of discovery: It *could* have been from Outer Space.

*

Krasnojarsk. Novosibirisk. Sverdlovsk. Needleman felt an irresistible buoyancy building inside him with each passing mile. In Noginsk, a Moscow suburb, the seed finally succumbed to his probings and unceremoniously fell to the floor.

Finally, there it was: the Scuteri seed—tangible affirmation of Needleman's sanity. Needleman knew that within that seed reposed all his insecurities and self-doubts. It was the physical embodiment of every flaw in his character.

The seed was putrid. A fetid bacterium had engulfed the seed by phagocytosis, and it smelled, when Needleman pressed the rancid kernel between his fingers, like death with bad breath. He was repulsed that this object had once been inside him. But he was done with the seed, once and for all. He took it between his fingers, rolled down the window, and flung it into the Unza River.

The seed had been expunged.

Nothing would ever be the same.

*

Needleman's newfound confidence appeared to suffuse Vijay, who drove with renewed determination. They flew through Poland, Germany and France, boarded a ferry from Le Havre to Portsmouth, drove on to Plymouth and booked passage on a freighter bound for the Brooklyn Navy Yards that, by pure chance, was setting sail just as they pulled into the port.

Finally docked in America, Vijay's gambit began to pay dividends. There was traffic on the Brooklyn Bridge, but it was traversable, and in under half an hour, they'd made it onto the FDR Drive. The FDR was crowded too, but passable, and in under 20 minutes they reached the 42nd Street exit. There was an accident on 42nd Street, but one could get by, and in merely 45 minutes, they'd made it over to Park Avenue. The Grand Central Station overpass had collapsed, but a short detour took them around the station, by way of Fifth Avenue. Fifth was also backed up, but they made steady progress, and in 20 minutes flat they'd covered the six blocks to 48th Street. Forty-eighth was closed, so Vijay dropped him off on the corner of Park and 50th. Needleman would walk the remaining two blocks.

He bounded out of the cab, brimming with enthusiasm. From now on, he'd take shit from no one. His proper name would be used. He'd be paid his full commissions. He would be treated with respect. Needleman paid the fare—$109,368.20 (including tolls, overages and a $20 tip) and leapt into his new life.

*

When Needleman walked into the office at 7:03, three minutes and 25 days late, the first person he saw was Lucas

Flounder, who appeared to be in one his moods. Flounder's clothes had been tailored for a man 30 pounds lighter. The too-tight shirts, grabbing waistlines, and confining braces restricted his blood flow, and when he was angry, which was often, cut off oxygen to his brain, and when he was really angry, as he appeared to be then, made him resemble an overripe melon.

"Get to work, Needleman," Flounder barked. "You look horrible. Did your mother forget to lay out clean clothes this morning?" The brokers looked up from their terminals and laughed.

Rage swelled inside Needleman. This was the moment for which he'd prepared. The nickname, the belittling jokes—everything would change. Tomorrow. Needleman knew better than to pick a fight when Flounder was in one of his moods. After 15 years, he could read Flounder like a book. Flounder wasn't merely mad that morning, he was super-super mad. The juice was about to spurt from his ears. No, this wasn't the right moment.

Needleman said simply, "Hello," and trudged to his

cubicle.

*

Stepping into a cab for the ride home, Needleman felt anxious. What did it mean that no one had noticed his three-week absence? Would the expense report for his cab ride be approved? His accounts had gone unattended during his hiatus; catching up would be daunting. To make matters worse, he'd accidentally jabbed his thumb with a pencil. He was sure a tiny splinter had become lodged in his finger, and though he'd scraped his skin raw, he couldn't extract the sliver.

Needleman slammed the door of the cab in anger. This misdirected sublimation made him angrier still. Then, to make matters worse, he heard the dreaded voice.

"This is Paul Sorvino. Actor, singer, chef, New Yorker, seatbelt wearer."

"77th and Columbus," Needleman said. "Take Sixth

Avenue."

The replying voice was unmistakable.

"We take park. It faster."

The Son Also Rises

In the waiting room of the Park Avenue offices of the renowned Dr. Milton Zion, Herb Ferrell leafed through the pile of magazines and mindlessly handed a copy of *Highlights for Children* to his son. As a child Herb had liked *Highlights*. It had easy mazes and connect-the-dots, simple tasks that even a young boy could manage. The magazine oozed familiarity. It had been fifty years since Herb's father had taken him to the pediatrician's office, but after all that time the magazine remained unchanged. The cover displayed the word "Highlights" in italics, then "for children" in print, one issue distinguishable from another only by color. Even the soft card stock remained unaltered. It had been the one tolerable aspect of visiting the doctor then, and so it was now. It pleased Herb Ferrell to pass this tradition, this bedrock, onto his son.

Jake accepted the magazine, leafed through it briefly, then set it back down in the pile of periodicals. He instead chose a copy of *The New Republic*, the cover of which rhetorically asked,

"The Politics of Genetics: Dare We Trust the New Gods?"

"I don't think you should be reading that," Herb said.

"It's okay," said his son. "I read *Commentary* too."

"I don't mean because of the politics; I mean because of the content."

The boy kept reading.

"I'm serious," Herb said sternly.

Jake pleaded with his eyes. "But Jed Perl wrote *The Diarist* this week. I love Jed Perl. And there's a review by Stanley Kauffman that I want to read."

"Stanley Kauffman can't still be the film critic," said Herb, surprised. "He must be more than eighty years old. Does anyone pay attention to what he has to say anymore?"

"Yes," Jake said. "He's an *achtung*-genarian."

"That's octogenarian," Herb corrected.

"I was making a joke."

Herb thought about it for a moment.

"I don't get it," he said.

"*Achtung*, the German word for attention," Jake

explained. "You said that no one paid attention to him anymore because he is too old. So, I called him an *achtung*-genarian, someone to whom attention must be paid."

He repeated, "Attention must be paid."

Jake did this occasionally, working lines from songs or plays into conversation. He particularly liked Arthur Miller. And Strindberg. Sometimes it put people off. Sometimes it put Herb off—most of the time really, this time included, but Herb realized too that it was important for him to hear it then. He needed to remember. Herb Ferrell didn't feel good about what he was doing—no parent would—but what choice did he have? Jake's transgression solidified Herb's resolve. He hoped they'd be called into the doctor's office soon.

"They should fill this area with water," Jake said, his face back in the magazine.

"Why is that?"

"Then it could be a wading room."

Herb gave a thin smile and wondered whether his

patience could last. Fortune shined upon him that day, though. No sooner did he doubt himself then a brown-haired woman with a well-nourished mole on her right cheek called out the name "Ferrell." A powerful sense of relief washed over Herb. It soothed him so much that he became agitated not at all when Jake shouted back, "Domesticated!" The other patients stared as father and son walked to meet the nurse. Some had looks of confusion on their faces; the older and younger Ferrell looked nothing like one another. The few that understood showed pity. Herb met all of their gazes with his head held high. He felt centered, self-possessed.

It would all be over soon.

The mole-woman led them slowly through the labyrinth of offices and examination rooms, painfully slowly, arriving finally at the doctor's office. A sign on the door said in bold capital letters: "MILTON ZION." Then underneath in smaller type: "PHYSICIAN." The nurse knocked, opened the door without waiting for an answer, and gestured for Herb and his son to enter.

It was a fine office, with dark wood paneling, plush carpet and a window that looked out to the street. From the proper angle, one could see Grand Central Station. The shelves had the right number of books, and just the right mix: mostly technical stuff, but a few general interest volumes that made the doctor seem human: a new Gore downer, Hawking's ruminations on time travel, a collection of Shel Silverstein cartoons. Diplomas lined the walls, and photographs too, lots of these, all with politicians and celebrities: Dr. Zion with Al Sharpton, Dr. Zion with Prince William. Democrats and Republicans, Jews and Muslims, Taiwanese and Chinese: all were represented here. Milton Zion drew no distinctions on the basis of ideology; he was a doctor for the masses. He greeted the Ferrells warmly: a firm handshake for Herb, for Jake a tussle of the hair.

"How are you feeling my boy?" he asked.

"I feel well and I feel good."

"Covering both the active and passive senses of the

question?"

"Right."

The doctor nodded and turned to the father. "IQ is still intact, I see."

"One hundred eighty and rising," Herb said. It was the sort of thing a parent should be proud of, but Herb Ferrell's voice had no hint of boast. To the contrary, he seemed put upon. But this wasn't Milton Zion's first rodeo. He didn't bite.

"Take a seat. Take a seat," the doctor said.

Herb sat down in one of the old-style wooden school chairs that sat upon the doctor's Oriental rug. Jake started to carry one of them away.

The doctor laughed heartily. "I mean sit down, Jake. Take a load off."

Jake returned the chair to its place.

"You know what they say," the boy said. "Chair today, gone tomorrow."

The doctor roared again, unnaturally in the view of Herb Ferrell, who turned to hide his cringe from his son.

"Very good, very good," Zion said. "You have quite the dry wit."

"The Republicans love me. They call me Bob Droll."

Herb winced, but the doctor shook his head and smiled again. He was eating this up.

"That's terrific," Zion said, "just terrific." He took a step towards Jake and pulled a tongue depressor and flashlight from his pocket. "Let me have a quick look."

After a fast "ah," and a look in the ears, Zion pulled out his stethoscope listened to Jake's heart.

"Sounds good," he said, concluding his examination. "You'll live to be one hundred."

"Spoken like a true Oracle," said Jake. "Or should I say ventricle?"

The doctor howled, and Jake too. Herb sat in silence, oblivious.

When the laughter subsided, Dr. Zion grew serious. "So what brings you here?"

"A taxi," Jake answered in a flash.

Herb showed his son his displeasure before he answered.

"It's the puns, doctor."

"What about them?"

"They're terrible. Half the time we don't even get them. The other half is worse"

"I find them to be quite creative."

"We don't."

Zion nodded. "Have you tried asking him to stop?"

"Nothing works. He can't help himself. They keep coming and coming."

"I'm like a great fighter," said Jake, punching the air with his fists. "I get knocked down but I get up again. I'm punacious."

Herb rolled his eyes. "It's like living at the Raleigh," he said.

Dr. Zion nodded his head solemnly. "It's probably just a stage."

"You don't understand. This goes on constantly."

"He's only three-and-a-half years old."

"Our patience is shot."

"Unfortunately, there's nothing that I can do about it."

Red in the face, Herb shot up from his chair. His wife had said that Zion would take this position, and so had prepared him for this moment. Herb calmed himself as best he could and turned to his son. "Jake," he said, "please excuse Dr. Zion and me."

"You're excused," said the boy.

"I'm serious."

"Has someone sneezed?"

"Jake, go outside and read a magazine until daddy is finished with the doctor."

"Why are you talking about yourself in the third person?"

"Jake," Herb said sternly.

The boy trudged out of the room.

"You know, you don't need to talk to me as if I'm three."

"Close the door behind you, son."

He did, leaving Herb and the doctor alone.

Herb sighed. "I don't think you appreciate the seriousness of this, Dr. Zion."

"I suppose I don't. The boy seems quite spectacular to me." He gave Herb a thin smile. "Frankly, I find the punning endearing."

Herb took a menacing step towards Dr. Zion. Herb Ferrell wasn't a strong man. He'd been a sickly boy and years of office work and gastric reflux disorder had rendered his gangly body stringier and his complexion, blanched as a child, downright gangrenous. But Milton Zion was no Atlas himself. When Herb Ferrell stood above the doctor, adrenaline surging through his body, he could sense Zion's intimidation.

Ethel Ferrell had said it would be this way. "If he did it to us, he's done it to others," she said. "He won't have the stomach to face you." Herb hadn't believed his wife, at first, but now he saw the truth of her insight, and drew strength from this. Though he'd risen in anger, he mastered himself, and spoke with restraint.

"You think his punning is endearing. Let me tell you a story, doctor: A few Sundays ago, my wife and I went to brunch with some friends. Our weekend housekeeper had called in sick that day and we weren't able to find a sitter, so we took Jake along. We knew the risk but we didn't have much of a choice. Besides, we figured it would be good for him to get out of the apartment.

"The meal started off fine. Jake sat quietly for the first half-hour. Then the food came. Jake ordered poached eggs. When they arrived, he began tapping his fist against his food.

"'What are you doing, Jake?' my wife asked.

"'Telling a knock-knock yolk,' he replied.

"'Please, son,' I said. 'not at the brunch table.'

"The boy said, 'I decided it was time for me to come out of my shell.' There was no stopping him after that.

"'Come on dad, stop egging me on.'

"'You've been coddling me for too long.'"

With each line, Herb took a step closer to Zion, his voice rising gradually.

"'Omletting you see the real me now.'

"'I'm using my egg-noggin to come up with these jokes.'

"'Are we going to just chalaza 'round here all day?'

"Stop! Stop! Stop!" Zion screamed. "They're terrible! I admit it! You'd have to be a doctor to understand the last one, and even then you might not get it. It doesn't follow from any of the others. It's gratuitous—punning for the sake of punning."

Herb stepped back from the doctor, satisfied, and sat down in his chair.

"All right," Zion said. "I see your point. But what do you want me to do?"

"I want you to make amends."

"I don't understand."

"I want you to set things right."

Dr. Zion spoke softly. He didn't want to raise Ferrell's ire again. "I hear what you're saying, Herb, and I understand that you and Susan are upset, but you got exactly what you asked for."

"This isn't what we asked for."

"You asked for a healthy boy," Milton Zion continued. "A healthy boy with a prodigious intelligence and a well-formed sense of humor. That's what you got."

"When we talked about the sense of humor, you said that you could make him sophisticated and urbane. You said you'd give him Woody Allen's wit—the good Woody Allen from *Annie Hall* and *Bananas* and *Take the Money and Run*—not the dour, introspective later version."

"This was just a point of comparison," Zion muttered.

"This isn't any version of Allen," said Herb Ferrell, his voice rising again. "It's not even the horrible *Interiors* version. You promised us a sardonic, intellectual Jewish sense of humor. Instead we got a British wit so dry it'd make *Monty Python* fans spit up their fish and chips, and not because they drown them in vinegar.

"He's a punner!" Herb exclaimed. "Even song parodists

thumb their noses at punners."

Herb sat back down. Dr. Zion waited for Herb to calm himself.

"Herb," he said, finally, "when you and Ethel came to see me five years ago, I explained to you that your expectations could only serve as general parameters. Genetic science has made incredible advances over the past decade. We can select for all sorts of traits—height, hair color, any of a myriad of personality characteristics. But how those different traits interact and manifest themselves in a real, living person isn't something anyone can predict. You and Ethel understood all of this."

Herb didn't flinch. "You promised us Woody Allen. You gave us Shecky Green. Living in my house is like living in the Catskills."

Milton Zion felt a headache coming on. "I still don't understand what you want me to do."

"I want you to correct the situation."

"How can I do that?"

"I think you know."

"I don't."

Herb Ferrell sat up straight in his chair. He didn't need to stand this time to intimidate the doctor.

"Do you know who I paid a visit to yesterday, Dr. Zion? Artie Weiss of Sterling & Lipton."

Milton Zion's headache felt worse. Instinctively, he reached for the analgesic powder he kept in his desk drawer.

"Attorney Weiss seems to think that Susan and I have a strong claim against you for breach of contract. He seems to think that we may be entitled to damages in excess of $10 million. And that doesn't include refund of the $700,000 fee we paid you."

"You signed a waiver," muttered Dr. Zion. "A two-hundred-forty-page waiver."

"Artie Weiss says he eats waivers like that for lunch."

It was true. Milton Zion had heard that Artie Weiss devoured waivers. And since no malpractice insurance covered this sort of business, many of his fellow doctors had been ruined by such lawsuits—ruined for following their own generous instinct to improve the human condition. Milton Zion hated lawyers. He made sure to repress the gene for litigiousness in all of his zygotes. Obviously it had fully expressed itself in Herb Ferrell's genetic makeup.

"It might be possible to do some gene therapy," said Zion, turning his hand upward in compromise. "We can try to deliver some therapeutic genes to the boy. We've had good success with this in many patients."

"Will that eliminate the condition?"

Milton Zion's forehead creased with earnestness. "Like I said, Herb, shaping personality isn't an exact science yet. It probably never will be. What I can do is inject genes that shape personality traits more in keeping with you and Ethel appear to want."

"But you can't say that it will eliminate the condition."

"It will make it better. Without a doubt it will make it much better."

"But not eliminate it?"

"It will abate it," said Zion, dropping his head, "but it cannot eliminate it."

"That's unacceptable."

Dr. Zion let out another long sigh. It was getting late. He and his wife had tickets for the opera—a 90-minute express version of Wagner's *Ring*, part of the new subscription series for busy professionals; the doctor worried now that he wouldn't make it on time. If he were late, his wife would berate him, which would make for the perfect ending to this utterly imperfect day. Zion wished he'd be called away to an emergency—anything to get his client or himself out of his office, but there were no emergencies in his line of work, just babies and test tubes. Herb Ferrell wouldn't disappear.

Zion rubbed his eyes. "I don't know what you want me to do, Herb," he said. "I can either try to make it better or we can leave things as they are. There are no other options."

The two men sat in silence. Milton Zion hoped for a moment that he had dissuaded Herb Ferrell from continuing down this ill-chosen path. But the father was only building up the courage to say what he had to say next.

"I want to return him," Ferrell said. "I want to return the boy."

Zion raised his eyebrows. "What do you mean?" he asked.

"You know exactly what I mean. I know it's possible. I want to return Jake."

"There's no such thing. You can't just give back a child. This isn't a department store. There are no refunds here."

Herb Ferrell stood up and moved in the doctor's direction again. He had no anger in his voice when he spoke this time, though, just the quiet resolve of a desperate man.

"I understand this isn't a shopping mall," Herb said. "On the other hand, I didn't exactly buy a $30 pair of khakis. My wife and I paid $700,000 for your services. I demand satisfaction. Either you give me what I or my attorney will have a judge put a sizeable dent in the Milton Zion Retirement Fund."

Herb stared at the doctor menacingly. "I think it would

be in both of our interests for you to accommodate me." He stared even harder. "You and I both know that what I am asking for is possible."

Indeed, the sad, scandalous truth was that it was possible.

Milton Zion didn't like to think about it. No one in his profession did. But there had been returns—more than a few—especially in the early days when the techniques hadn't yet been perfected: boys designed to be young Mozarts—pianists and composers, who found themselves inclined instead to tin cans and tables and other percussives; girls invested with all the gifts for figure skating and gymnastics who wasted their time playing at jacks and hopscotch, squandering their endowments on unsuspecting seven-year-olds who couldn't compete with their quickness and sharp reflexes; all sorts of would-be prodigies who grew into nothing more than ordinary little boys and girls, all to the great consternation of their parents. The troubling precedent for dealing with these genetic disappointments had been established early on: the seminal case of Z.

Z wasn't known to the general public, but in the relevant medical sub-community one couldn't find a doctor who didn't know of, and have an opinion on, his case. The physicians who created Z tweaked all of the artistic genes in the fertilized egg—genes for acuity of vision and sensitivity to environment and color. The resulting child would be a modern Michelangelo, the doctors told the parents. This mostly satisfied them, though Z's mother expressed her wish that some of Monet's tenderness be mixed in; she had always fancied the water lilies. The doctors said they would oblige. The baby would have all of that, they said, and more too.

But when the amalgam of chromosomes became a real boy, the product disappointed. It showed no interest in watercolors or sculpture or any of the fine arts. The young boy only had an eye for comic books, which he devoured ravenously. His taste knew no sensibilities or bounds: the manly X-Men, the effete Richie Rich, he liked them all equally well. He sketched with striking ingenuity. His boldest creation: a hermaphroditic anti-hero that took the shape of its target's deepest fantasy, then copulated relentlessly with the victim until the person began to spill blood where life should have flowed; when the unsuspecting prey finally noticed, it was too late for them to be saved.

Some might have seen genius there, but not Mr. & Mrs. Z. The entire enterprise shamed them—the juvenile picture books and macabre sketches spread all over their son's floor— they wouldn't allow guests to enter their home. This wasn't the sort of behavior their friends would understand or that the parents themselves had expected when they plunked down $500,000 for what Mr. Z referred to as gene insurance.

When little Z reached the age of three and the symptoms showed no signs of abating, the couple returned to the scientists in exasperation. The doctors poked and prodded and tried to figure where they had gone wrong, but it was as Milton Zion had told Herb—not even the top doctors could predict the end product. Science had made tremendous strides in the ten years since Z's case, but predicting how genes would interact would always be, in some part, guesswork. Mr. & Mrs. Z had been told this in advance—just as Herb Ferrell and his wife had been, and they were told it again at the time of their complaint. But it didn't assuage the Z's at all. They'd paid lots and lots of money, and they demanded satisfaction.

So, quietly, Z's doctors arranged for the baby to be taken off his parents' hands. They couldn't just put it up for adoption, of course. In time the adoptive parents would ask questions about the child; this would raise too great a risk of discovery of his origin. The governments of the world still looked unfavorably on genetic tinkering, especially the United States. In private, congressmen and chancellors alike sought out the expertise of genetic "counselors" for their not-yet-conceived children. In public, though, they condemned genetic engineering as immoral. Too unpredictable, they said. Too much like playing God. This was what the people wanted to hear, so this is what they said. It would be decades before the law would permit anything of this kind. In the interim the politicians and scientists reached an unspoken accommodation: no one would limit the geneticists' work so long as they kept things quiet. If they failed to maintain their silence, no promises could be made. So Z's doctors moved clandestinely.

The doctors sent Z to the isthmus of Kalaupapa on the Hawaiian island of Molokai. Kalaupapa had been a Hansen's Disease colony once. High sea cliffs isolated it from the rest of the island, making the location ideal for this purpose. It was ideal in other respects, too. Long after doctors brought leprosy under control with sulfa drugs the residents of the colony remained, choosing to spend the remainder of their days in the splendor of the island, rather than struggling to integrate themselves into mainstream society, which they knew only through television and magazines.

By the time Z arrived, the former lepers had all died, leaving behind a tiny, isolated paradise, and just enough of an infrastructure to accommodate the needs of several dozen children. Z was the first, though others quickly followed. Soon the colony swelled with boys and girls—genetic blunders—and their keepers. In time life on Molokai settled into something resembling normal—a community of gifted but flawed orphans living among the oddly misplaced relics of their predecessors. They took their classes in a schoolroom that had holes cut into the floor to accommodate the uncontrollable spitting characteristic of Hansen's Disease. On their way to class each day they passed a 1983 Toyota Corolla, the peninsula's only car, which the leper Carol Sakai had bought with money earned from 46 years of knitting wool socks. In her day, she drove it proudly each morning from her home to her shop, a distance of exactly one-fourteenth of a mile, then back again to her hut at five o'clock. The orphans knew nothing of this, of course—Carol Sakai died long before Z and the others arrived; the car was just another of the many peculiarities of their environment. Years later, they harnessed the engine of the car to power an electron microscope, which they constructed from a pair of reading glasses belonging to Father Damien, the patron saint of lepers. This was but one example of the remarkable ingenuity the children displayed with the scarce resources available to them.

What little they had come from the geneticists, who supported the misfits' teachers and caretakers and paid for the scant supplies. Some of Z's doctors set up a foundation for the island under the ironic name, Kid's First. At first these scientists were the only contributors, but as the ranks of pariah children grew so too did the roster of donors, almost all of whom contributed out of shame, like a butter manufacturer contributing to the American Heart Association, a john to AIDS research.

Nobody discussed the island. According to the U.S. government, Kalaupapa had been deserted when the last of the remaining lepers, 93-year old Roy Nishikawa, died at the turn of the millennium. Some native Hawaiians doubted the official reports—they could see activity on the island from their fishing boats. But no one went to investigate. Though leprosy had been brought under control more than 50 years earlier, no one dared take the chance. The secret of the island remained safe.

Soon, though, word leaked out only in the medical

community: a hushed word at a cocktail party, a drunken confession from one physician to another, an oblique reference on the golf course. Milton Zion had learned of the colony five years earlier when he asked a colleague what had become of a particularly interesting patient the two men had once discussed: a young boy designed for politics who, at the age of three, developed a phobia of having his hand touched. The colleague told Zion that the boy had improved and was doing well, but Zion could see from his friend's troubled expression that he hadn't told the entire truth. Two days later, the friend called back, and asked if he and Zion could have dinner that night, during which the doctor confessed. He felt it important for Zion to know he said, "in case the need ever arose."

Now the need had arisen. Zion knew there would be no sense in contradicting Herb Ferrell. Zion could only guess how he knew—probably from his relentless attorney, but it made no difference. He knew the truth and that was that. There'd be no changing his mind at this point.

So he nodded in silent agreement. He hated the idea of

the colony. These children had done nothing to deserve being cast out. They posed no threat to others. It was barbaric to send them away. Zion had always said that he wouldn't succumb to this solution if, heaven forbid, the situation ever presented itself. But now that he was in it, he saw no other choice.

This is what it means to get old, Zion thought to himself—to compromise the sense of who you believe you are. For an entire life one swears that there are things he'll never do—employ a housekeeper, join a country club, own a sub-zero refrigerator, but then the need arises and you wonder not just how you ever got by without these things and why you ever vowed to deprive yourself. In the heat of the moment, Milton Zion saw no alternative course of action. If he resisted, he'd be put out of business. Thousands of other parents would be deprived of his services and their fondly received miracles. Furthermore, he was exhausted. If he capitulated, he might be able to make it to the opera in time, and be spared his wife's venom.

"Okay," Zion sighed. "I'll take care of it."

Tension seeped out of Herb Ferrell's body as if it had been released from a clogged drain. "Thank you," he said. "Thank you very much. We don't want to make any trouble, my wife and I. Especially not Ethel—she wouldn't hurt a fly—she couldn't even bring herself to come here today. But, as you see, the situation is intractable."

Milton Zion held his hand up. "I said I'd take care of it."

"Thank you. Thank you again."

"When do you want to do it?"

"I don't understand."

"When do you want to drop Jake off?"

The question flustered Herb Ferrell. "I thought," he stammered, "I thought I could just leave him here."

"He really does think it's a department store," Zion thought to himself, wondering whether it were possible to live with any living creature for three years—even a goldfish, and not form some attachment. But the doctor didn't express his incredulity or his offense aloud. This would lead only to another round of accusations and threats and the repeated invocation of the name of Artie Weiss. Zion couldn't bear the thought of this. They had a cot in one of the back rooms. The boy could sleep there. They could pull in the television from the nurse's station to keep him company. Zion would take care of the other arrangements in the morning.

"No problem," he said. "I just thought you might like to say goodbye."

The doctor's words hit Herb Ferrell hard; farewells hadn't occurred to him. In his mind and during the many conversations in which he and his wife had gone over what might happen when Herb confronted Zion they'd never gotten past the point of agreement. He felt no great desire to say goodbye to his son, but at the same time he didn't want to appear insensitive. "Perhaps just a word," Herb said. "I don't want to make it harder on Jake with a long goodbye."

Zion nodded. "I understand," he said. Then he pressed a button on his intercom and said, "Could you bring Jake back in here?"

The nurse produced the boy quickly, half-shoving him into the doctor's office with a palpable look of relief upon her face. She hurried out of the room, not waiting to be excused.

"It's all right," Jake said, turning to his father. "I've come back."

Arthur Miller again. Herb knew there'd be a spate of puns. There always were whenever the boy had been deprived of attention for any length of time. He could imagine what that nurse had been through.

Jake smiled—he always did at his own jokes. "Like Napoleon before me—back from exile," he said. Then, in an Arnold Schwarzenegger voice, he added, "Ell be back."

Herb shook his head. In that instant, whatever doubts had lingered in his mind dispersed like a vapor. The situation was truly unmanageable.

"Jake," Herb heard himself say, "You're going to stay here with Dr. Zion tonight."

Jake thought about this, and Herb worried that the boy

would protest or that he would ask questions, to which Herb
hadn't developed answers. But after a few seconds the familiar
smile returned to Jake's face, and Herb Ferrell knew that his son
hadn't been bothered at all; he was merely thinking of something
witty to say.

Jake smiled. "It'll be like making Aliyah," he said.

"I don't get it."

"You know," the little boy grinned, "spending a night in
Zion."

Herb felt the familiar sour feeling in his stomach, but this
wasn't the time to express his displeasure. Instead he ruffled the
boy's hair and said, "That's great, Jake – very funny." Then,
taking a step toward the door he said to Zion, "Well, I'll leave
the two of you then." And without another word he stepped out
of the doctor's office – and out of his son's life.

It had been a mistake to run his hand through Jake's
hair. Jake had begun talking at the age of four months, and the
puns started soon thereafter. From that point forward, Herb

almost never touched his son. Asking Jake to stay with Dr. Zion hadn't bothered the boy. His father's touch, however, aroused his alarm. As Herb walked out of the office, Jake had a palpable expression of horror, as if he had figured everything out in that instant when finger touched hair, which he probably had, precocious as he was. Herb regretted this—both for Jake and for himself—because it had made things harder than they needed to be.

But as Herb Ferrell stepped out onto Park Avenue, his face splashed by the crisp air of the season, he felt no pangs of regret. He didn't feel at all like a man who'd just left his son behind since, as he reminded himself, Jake wasn't his son in any meaningful sense. Those weren't only Herb and Ethel Ferrell's natural genes in there. Instead, he'd been built out of a concoction of chromosomes and DNA that a scientist had brewed with centrifuges and microneedles under the lens of a microscope. Herb was a father to Jake as much as he was a father to the family poodle or to the dust mites on his pillow. They'd lived together for a time, not a very long time at that, and now that time had come to an end.

Herb Ferrell felt no sadness or regret. Rather he felt like a man who'd ended a relationship with a girlfriend that had long before gone bad. He felt relief and an overwhelming sense of possibility.

They'd tried to do too much with Jake. The scientists had almost no track record with more abstract personality traits, such as senses of humor. And the Ferrells had asked for not just any sense of humor, but one to rival the sharpest wit known to man. This time, they wouldn't make the same mistakes.

Herb and Ethel had already begun discussing their new child. Herb wanted a chess player. He'd wanted one the first time, but Ethel had won out with Jake. This time Herb would get his way, and he'd learned his lesson well. They wouldn't ask for the new boy to be a world champion or anything like that, just good enough to be a grandmaster by seven or eight, which was really nothing in this day and age. Nor would they complicate the mix, as they had before. They'd ask only for a few additional traits. Ethel insisted that the new boy be a mellifluous tenor and have a taste for watercolors and a fine sense of direction. The new doctor they had consulted assured them that this wouldn't be a problem.

"We're already cooking the stew," he said.

Herb Ferrell smiled at the thought and took a long, deep breath of the autumn air. He felt vibrant and alive.

Soon he would be a father.

Waiting for the Cable Guy

When the phone rang shortly after four o'clock, the man known on Earth as Franklin Burns expected that it would be someone from the cable company calling to explain where their man had been all day and offering appropriate apologies. The appointment had been set a month earlier, by a company agent who decreed—without inquiry into its convenience, that an installer would stop by on the 23rd, between eight AM and five PM.

"That's a nine-hour window," Frank protested at the time. "Can't you give me something earlier?"

"No," she said. "We're booked solid. That's the earliest appointment we have."

"But it's not an appointment in any meaningful sense of the word. It's at best a vague commitment. You're not being specific."

"We're telling you the day. We're being specific about that."

"If we had a date for lunch, and I said, 'I'll meet you at McDonald's between eight and five,' would you consider that an appointment?"

"I would never eat at McDonald's."

"Forget the restaurant. Would it be an appointment?"

"I'm not authorized to have semantic debates. Do you want the appointment?"

"I vehemently object to the term."

"All the same."

"What's my alternative?"

"We could have someone come by on the 30th between eight and five."

"I'll take the 23rd on condition that we not classify this as an appointment."

"I'm not authorized to enter into stipulations."

"All right, fine," Frank said, hanging up in anger. More than anything else, it bothered Frank that the agent presumed he had no commitments or appointments or a job that might have precluded him from waiting around his apartment for nine hours. In fact, he didn't have any of these conflicts, but the agent couldn't have known this.

Frank stewed about the conversation for the following four weeks; still he might've called it even if the installer had showed up early on the appointed day. Alas, the installer didn't show up in the early morning. Nor did he show up in the mid-morning or the late morning or the early afternoon. The waiting might've been bearable if he could've watched TV, but of course, this wasn't possible, so Frank instead spent the day pacing his apartment, working himself into a frenzy. By 3PM, he could feel the blood pulsing through his system with such force that he thought each heartbeat might generate an aneurysm.

When the phone rang another hour later, Frank felt certain it would be the cable company's president calling to make amends. At this point, common decency required that the company offer apologies from the highest levels, and grant Frank several months of free service, or least a few gratis pay-per-view movies. But it wasn't the cable company calling to apologize—it was his mother.

"So, you haven't called in two days." Frank's mother greeted him by his birth name, which could neither be spelled nor pronounced in English. His people used a symbolic language; his name wouldn't have been recognized on Earth, except in Japan where it resembled the character for laxative.

"I've asked you before not to call me by that name on this line."

"What, a mother can't call her son by his own name?"

"Look, Mom, I need to keep the phone free. I'm waiting for a call."

"Who's so important? The prime minister of the United States?

"No," Frank winced. "The cable company."

"And this cable company is more important than your mother? I thought you went to Earth to study TV. All of a sudden you're studying rope?"

"I don't have time to explain now. Call me back later."

"'His mother calls from 7,000 light years away and he

says, 'call me back later.'"

"Mom, please."

"So when are you going to call Elsa Colodny? I saw her grandmother at the pool. The girl is waiting by the phone for your call. She just started podiatry school, you know."

His mother never relented. She was always on his case to call this one's niece or that one's daughter. The matchmaking might not have been so bad if she didn't insist on fixing him up with Brotonarians, who Frank found to be judgmental and overbearing and who frowned on eating shellfish. A psychologist might have classified this behavior as self-loathing, but Frank liked shellfish, and that was that. Frank had hoped that some distance might lead his mother to ease off, but even 7,000 light years hadn't done the trick. It drove Frank crazy, but he didn't have time for an argument.

"Let's talk about it later, Mom."

"Death is soon. Everything else is later."

"Goodbye, Mom."

"Goodbye, son. If I die while you're abroad, please come home for the funeral."

"Yes, Mom. I'm hanging up now."

Frank tried to decompress. He'd explained to his mother countless times that each call created a risk of detection. It was a small risk—the danger would be realized only if a microwave radiation detector happened to be pointed at his home planet at the precise moment of the call. But it was a risk all the same, and if by some chance Earth scientists did detect the communication, his university's Institutional Review Board would immediately suspend all Earth research projects. Every graduate student in the galaxy knew how dogmatic IRBs had become. Frank would have to pack up, go home, and start his dissertation from scratch. This would be disastrous to his academic career. Of course, it would suit his mother just fine.

Frank breathed deeply and counted to ten. The cable company's delay had kept him from working on his dissertation, and he'd filled the time studying Eckhart Tolle, whose teachings he now put in practice. As the tension seeped from his body, his focus shifted to a more practical concern: since he didn't have call waiting he had no way of knowing if the cable company had called while he was on with his mother. Call waiting cost five dollars a month, which is serious money on a graduate student's budget. Statistically speaking, it was unlikely the company had called while he was on with his mother, but it was possible. He stared at the phone, willing it to ring. Then, inevitably, he considered calling the cable company.

Frank already had called 17 times that day. Twelve of these had ended with his call being dropped after a long wait on hold, and none of the five calls that went through had produced any information—rather, they'd only annoyed the omnipotent simpletons in the scheduling department, who had the capacity to ensure that an installer never arrived, not that day or any other, and that Frank would spend his entire graduate school career locked in a studio apartment reading self-help books. But surely they wouldn't be offended by his asking whether they'd called while he was on the phone. Frank paced back and forth, nervously fidgeting with his earlobe implant. His brain said he shouldn't call. His heart said he should.

Frank went with his heart. As soon as he dialed, the familiar Warnervision jingle greeted him. A recorded voice began to explain the menu options, but Frank knew the drill. He confidently pressed keys: one for English, five for people with existing accounts, then his 13-digit account number, six to schedule or confirm an appointment, then two for customers with an existing appointment. The system didn't offer the option of speaking to a representative, but Frank knew to press zero, which took him to another menu. He pressed three to schedule or confirm an appointment, two to confirm an appointment, re-entered his 13-digit account number, pressed zero, and then waited. Once per minute during this period a phone line rang. On the first 25 of these occasions, a recorded message told him that his call was very important to Warnervision, that they were experiencing "extraordinary call volume," and to please be patient. On the 26th ring, a human being answered.

"Warnervision, this is Mrs. Harrison. Can I help you?"

On three of Frank's five prior successful calls, he'd spoken with Mrs. Harrison. He wasn't sure how to play this. On the one hand, persistence might make his case more sympathetic. On the other hand, Mrs. Harrison might regard him as pesty. On the third hand, she probably fielded hundreds of calls each day, and might appreciate a gentle reminder that his case deserved attention.

"Hello," Frank said, in his saccharine telephone voice. "I called a bit earlier to check on my appointment for this afternoon."

"What's your account number, please?" Frank knew better than to question why she didn't have the number even though he'd already keyed it in twice. He'd wasted an entire call with a Mr. Bettis, exploring why the agent couldn't access the account number or, if he couldn't, why Frank had been asked to enter the information in the first place. Bettis responded that they were experiencing high call volume, which couldn't be avoided. Eckhart Tolle's teachings notwithstanding, Frank became enraged. He deemed Bettis's response irrelevant and rejected the premise that call volume on a random Tuesday could be unusually high. This triggered Bettis to initiate a protocol for irate clients, which consisted principally of saying, "Please calm down," but served only to further ire Frank, who continued debating Bettis until, finally, his call was dropped. Frank could never verify his suspicion that this had been purposeful, but the specter of a call being again dropped—and having to repeat the elaborate keying ritual—loomed over every interaction with Warnervision, and Frank yielded his number without protest.

"Ah, hello, Mr. Burns."

This raised Frank's antennae. Several possible inferences could be drawn from the "ah," none of which were good. At the very least, Mrs. Harrison recalled her earlier conversation with Frank, which didn't bode well. Worse, it might suggest that Bettis had discussed him with the entire office. Frank envisioned a bullpen of agents, who ridiculed the most persistent customers and resolved to make life difficult for them. It would go a long way to explaining the telephone delays.

"I was on the phone briefly. Did you call?"

"No."

"Well, while I have you, do you have an update on my appointment?

"No, sir."

"How can that be?"

"We told you that the installer would be there between eight A.M. and five P.M."

"It's almost four thirty."

"Last time I checked, four thirty comes before five o'clock."

Frank had the receiver in a death grip. "Can you at least confirm that I'm next on the list?"

"I cannot, sir."

"Well, then at least you could now say that he will be late."

"No, sir. The dispatcher gives the installers a list each morning. We have no way of telling where they are on the list."

"Can we at least say that it's now likely that he'll miss the agreed-upon window?"

"There's a lot of traffic, Mr. Burns, as I'm sure you know."

"You should be able to account for that in advance."

"Traffic's outside of our control."

"Traffic may be outside of your control, but budgeting for traffic isn't outside your control!" He was shouting now. "You can't just fail to account for traffic and then, when your people are late day after day, call it an act of God. It's like an airline failing to allocate time in its schedules for landings and takeoffs. There's always traffic! Just schedule fewer appointments."

Mrs. Harrison didn't answer for a while. Frank understood this meant she was debating between dropping the call and implementing the enraged-client protocol.

"I'm sorry, sir. Traffic's outside of our control."

"Is that what your training manual tells you to say? Do you understand it doesn't respond to my point? Customers aren't morons!" He was aware of the risk, but this needed to be said.

This was the core problem with earthlings. They'd evolved all kinds of defense mechanisms—religion, fate, biological determinism—to evade responsibility for their actions. It was a shame because the planet had some wonderful television programming.

His comments hung in the air until finally Mrs. Harrison said, "I'm sorry, sir, but the issue is outside of out control."

Frank shuddered.

"What about the list?" he asked, more calmly. "Can you just tell me what number I am and what number you're up to?"

"I don't have that. The dispatcher gives it directly to the installer."

"Why don't you have a copy?"

"It wouldn't be of any use to us, sir"—Frank presumed the use of "sir" was part of the protocol. "Some appointments take longer than others, and, because of traffic, it's impossible to predict travel time. We have no way of predicting where the installer is on the list."

"Why don't you have the dispatcher call in after every appointment? He must have a cell phone. This way you'd always know where he was. Then, instead of making customers wait all day you could call them when the installer was close."

This comment met silence on the other end. Frank hoped she was mulling over what he had said, but he couldn't be sure.

"Are you there, Mrs. Harrison?"

"It's outside our control, sir. If the installer isn't there before five o'clock, we'll reschedule for another day."

What would be the point of that? Why schedule another vague appointment, which the company would fail to honor? For that matter, why have a customer service department that existed solely to frustrate customers? And, while they were putting things on the table, why live life if it was nothing more than the unfolding of a pre-written drama? Frank knew better than to ask these questions, though. Nothing would come of it. He muttered a word of thanks, hoping Mrs. Harrison might have some mercy on him, meekly hung up the phone, and despaired.

The universe once had been at his fingertips. He'd attended the best schools: Bolotrusatrusa Prep and Teetabalabalaroosta University, in the days when it was still exclusively Brotonarian. Inevitably, the school caved to cultural pluralism, and let in all kinds, though it remained primarily Brotonarian. They served milk and palaroot in the dining halls at the same time, which once would have been unthinkable, and ran the elevators on Shibday. With a glass or three of wine in them, some professors would cite this as evidence that Teetabalabalaroosta had lost its way. But Frank's credentials were impeccable—he finished top in his class and earned distinction for his thesis in psycho-sociology.

With his academic record, he could've written his ticket to a top medical school or law school. Instead, he chose to get his Ph.D. This crushed his mother. In the best-case scenario, he'd land a low-paying professorship. He'd be a glorified teacher. Whatever people might say publicly about the importance of education, they privately looked down at teachers. His mother took the entire thing personally. Since he was born, she'd been campaigning for him to be a doctor and she took his decision, not entirely without basis, as a rejection of her.

Choosing to study on Earth only made matters worse. Even Frank's professors questioned this choice. The Kilimangahelians had low regard for the planet. Like anyplace else, Earth had its redeeming qualities. They sold these little tins of pudding, which came with their own plastic spoon. The Kilimangahelians liked pudding very much. But the spoon tended to snap when one pried it loose, and, truth be told, it hardly made sense to travel halfway across the galaxy for even the most delicious pudding. More damningly, earthlings appeared to be hell bent on destroying their planet by superheating it with carbon.

But Frank had great faith in the people of Earth and his dissertation, provisionally titled: *Through a Scanner Brightly: Omnisexual Motifs in Earth-American Situational Comedy Television.* Cluck's Theory of Specific Sexual Evolution had become so widely accepted that it hardly made sense to call it a theory. He'd shown that as a species ascended Kornberg's stages of development—from primitive to technological to space-faring and, finally, to post-sentient—its sexuality concurrently evolved. Inevitably, post-sentient species were omnisexual. More controversially, Cluck hypothesized that species pre-consciously recognized these changes. For this he'd been branded a quack, and Frank's committee chair strongly discouraged him from pursuing this idea, but Frank wouldn't be deterred.

Though humans were centuries away from interplanetary space travel, he found compelling evidence that they'd begun to explore their latent sexuality in the early boy-boy comedy teams—Abbott and Costello, Laurel and Hardy, Gleason and Carney in *The Honeymooners*. Could there have been less passion in the kisses Ralph Kramden forced upon Alice, or more tension with Norton? Time and again, American sitcoms showed preconscious libidinal confusion: Don Knotts in the *Andy Griffith Show*, *Mister Ed*'s Wilbur, who spent more time with his horse than his beautiful wife, and the entire bizarre plot of *Green*

Acres. The intrepid captain of *The Love Boat*, Merrill Stubing, seemed to have scant interest in love himself. What was between the Skipper and Gilligan and Felix Unger and Oscar Madison?

Frank proposed to study American television during a critical time in human evolution: the 1980s, when the effete Mister Bentley paraded around *The Jeffersons* and Max Klinger wore dresses on *M*A*S*H*, well past the point when it had any relevance to the show. Frank loved *M*A*S*H* so much he took his Earth name from the show. The decade also covered the seminal *ALF*. No relationship displayed the complexity of human sexuality so much as that between the title character and his benefactor, Willie.

Even after his dissertation committee grudgingly approved the project, Frank encountered resistance from the institutional review board. Generally speaking, IRBs were reluctant to approve on-site research on planets with which contact hadn't yet been established. The board asked why Frank couldn't do this from home. They had advanced satellite dishes on Kilimanganahelia, after all. You could get over 20,000 channels from hundreds of different planets, including Earth. It was though channel surfing that Frank had discovered Earth and piloted his study.

The dishes weren't good enough, Frank said. Some stations came through scrambled. Rain, snow, and anything that obstructed a clear southern view blocked reception. How many times had he been in the middle of a crucial program when he saw that dreaded message, "Searching for Satellite Signal?" This charge resonated with the IRB members, who'd experienced it in their own homes—even the top Kilimanganahelian scientists couldn't remedy the problem.

Frank bolstered his case with an emotional appeal. True, Earth remained barbaric in many ways. It hadn't yet conquered sickness and hunger. They waged war in the name of religion and sometimes committed genocide. But they had great potential. If, as Frank had, the committee members had watched Earth's children grow up on *Saved by the Bell* and *Charles in Charge*, and seen them grow old, as they did with such grace in *The Golden*

Girls, they'd share his faith in humanity.

The IRB grudgingly agreed, but cut his budget to the bone. They authorized funds for *HBO*, but not for *Cinemax* or *Showtime*. They required him to use a conventional, 21-inch TV rather than the high-definition flat screen he requested. They might as well have transported him by horse and carriage, he said. How could he appreciate the subtlety of *Seinfeld* without hi-def? Basic necessities only, the board said, take it or leave it. Frank took it.

So now he sat in his tiny Lower East Side studio, above a take-away Chinese restaurant, the smell of Moo Goo Gai Pan wafting through the air, starting at his wall clock, one of those three-dollar IKEA jobs that works just fine and makes you wonder, on the one hand, why anyone ever spends more on a clock and, on the other, how your life went so horribly wrong that you can't afford a nicer one. He'd stared at it for so long that its hands appeared to be moving backward. It was 4:45. In fifteen minutes, *The King of Queens* would come on—a pivotal episode in which Doug fears that he's delivered a bomb. Soon thereafter, his mother would call to pester him again about Elsa Colodny and berate him for wasting his life. When she called, he wanted to be able to say honestly that he was working. The installation process took only ten minutes, If the installer came in the next five minutes, he'd finish in time.

The minute hand moved. Frank stared at the door buzzer, willing it to ring, then turned away from the buzzer, thinking it'd be more likely to ring if he didn't stare at it.

When he tired of starting or not staring at the buzzer, he crumbled up sheets of loose-leaf paper and shot them at the garbage can in the kitchen, which was really just a sink and a hotplate placed in the corner of the apartment. Frank told himself that if he made three in a row, the buzzer would ring. He made three in a row. The buzzer still didn't ring.

At 4:56, it occurred to Frank that his buzzer might not be working. He had no specific reason to think this. A delivery person successfully had rung up two days earlier. But things break, especially in New York City, and the superintendent of his building wasn't exactly on top of things. If Frank had been diligent, he would've checked it that morning. Perhaps the installer already had rung the bell. Perhaps he was downstairs even now, waiting to be let up. Frank considered running down, but this would mean abandoning the phone. The safer bet would be to call the cable company.

He dialed the number and raced through the litany— one, five, the account number, six, two, wait a moment, zero, three, two, the account number again, zero. This time Frank heard the special ring straight away. He'd been connected directly to the customer service department. For a moment, Frank became hopeful.

Then he heard the message: "Thank you for calling the Warnervision customer service division. The department is currently closed for the day. Your call is very important to us. Please call back tomorrow at 9AM." Frank planned to leave a message for Harrison and Bettis that they'd left four minutes early and the jig was up, but there was no beep, just a disconnecting click. Frank returned to staring at the wall.

When the phone rang at precisely five o'clock, his heart didn't leap. They'd finally broken him. He no longer hoped that it would be the cable company president calling to apologize. He knew better. He knew precisely who it would be and precisely what he'd say.

"Hi, Mom. I'll take Elsa Colodny's number now."

Nosferatu Rabinowitz Turns 60

The doorbell rang and Nos, awakening with a start, hit his head on the coffin. "Damn," he said to himself. "Damn. Damn. Damn." It was as if there were a massive conspiracy to keep him from getting a good night's sleep. The principal problem was his prostate. At a minimum, he woke up five times a night to pee, and that was if he didn't drink for three hours before bedtime. If he allowed himself so much as a sip of water he'd wake up even more often. One time, he woke up eleven times in a single night. Imagine waking up eleven times! After the eighth or ninth, it hardly seems worth the effort to fall back asleep. The logistical difficulties of his sleeping arrangements only made a bad situation worse. He couldn't simply get up and go to the bathroom like everyone else. Over the years, Nos had tried almost everything imaginable, but finally settled on the simplest solution—an empty Motts Apple Juice bottle, which he kept with him in the sanctum. He hated that damned bottle. Using it required him to contort himself like a pretzel, and the smell was murder. There was no circulation at all in the coffin.

Nos was stubborn, but even he had a limit, and after several years of living like this, he capitulated and sought out a doctor. Finding one was nearly impossible. The only urologist he could find who both accepted his insurance and maintained evening hours was in Chinatown, which meant a 40-minute subway ride on the B. Nos hated the B. He almost turned back around to Brooklyn when he saw the doctor's office was located over a Chinese restaurant, and then again when he found 36 people in the waiting room. But Nos was desperate, so much so that he endured even the anal exam without protest.

Dr. Haichao Wang was mercifully efficient, and when he finished probing, he handed Nos a prescription for Flomax and said in the thickest Chinese accent, "game changer—game changer." Nos tried to probe him about the drug, but Wang didn't speak much English. They'd gotten through the exam with pointing and hand gestures. To each question, Wang replied, "Game changer—game changer." He said "game changer" so many times it made Nos cringe, and on the trek back to Brooklyn he thought several times of throwing the prescription away, but he was at his wit's end, and had the prescription filled at the CVS on Neptune Avenue.

Wang was right; it was a game changer. His condition gradually improved. That day, his 60th birthday, he'd only awoken twice, and had slept for four straight hours for the first time in as long as he could remember. Imagine, then, his frustration at being awoken by the doorbell! Nos checked the battery-powered digital clock he kept in the corner of the coffin. It read 7:33. He couldn't arise for another 37 minutes. Some people loved Daylight Savings Time, but to him it was a nightmare—or day-mare, if you will. Imagine not being able to start one's day until half past eight o'clock in the evening! Nos consoled himself with the thought that at this hour it was unlikely the business was of any consequence. Besides, he could use more sleep. Nos prophylactically peed in the Motts bottle, dropped his head to the pillow and slipped off into one of those luscious pre-sunset snoozes.

As soon as he dozed, it seemed, the doorbell rang again. It truly was a conspiracy! What could possibly be so important? He checked the time again: 8:16. Nos sighed. There was no avoiding the day now. Slowly, he opened coffin lid, allowing his eyes time to adjust. Nos always took his time waking up. Heart attacks were three times more likely to occur in the morning than the evening—he figured the reverse applied to him. Gathering his strength, he placed his palms flat on the base of the coffin and raised his torso. Then, he swung his legs over the side and, finally, in a single swift movement simultaneously lifted his body while swinging his legs to the floor. At last, he was standing.

Behold Nosferatu Aaron Rabinowitz!

Truth was, he felt awful. Every part of his body ached. He had cramps in both his legs. His right foot was still asleep. His lower back was in agony. As he gulped down the dregs of last night's coffee, trying to shake his torpor, he wondered yet again whether he'd ever get a decent night's sleep. Even before his prostate problems, it was impossible to spend restful night in that coffin. He couldn't find a comfortable position. Most of the time, he slept with his knees under his chin. For years he'd been promising himself to buy a larger casket but money was tight, and with the economy being what it was, it didn't seem like the right time to be making major improvements. How many times had his mother told him to save for a rainy day? Saving money was a way to honor her.

Nos took a sip of cold Chock Full o'Nuts. "No," he said to himself. "If you can't be honest with yourself, then you can't be honest with anyone." A sixtieth birthday is one of those red-letter days that encourage reflection. Nos felt a sudden resolve to speak with candor. "Tell the real story of the coffin," he said to himself.

The real story of the coffin began in the heart of the rainforest, 58 years earlier, when Nos, known then as Menachem, was just two years old. His mother's brother, Ira, a Lubavitch on mission in the Amazon, was in the Nukak Tunahi region, trying to convert some pygmies, when he sampled some native tea. Unbeknownst to Ira, the tea contained traces of

Jurema root bark. Unbeknownst to the pygmies, Lubavitch Jews are extremely allergic to dimethyltryptamine, and pretty much everything else. Uncle Ira went into anaphylactic shock and died.

The Mbuti pygmies generously carried out the body and in two days' time Ira was back in the U.S. He'd never married, and so the duty fell to Nos's mother to make funeral arrangements. She purchased a coffin, a burial plot and booked time at Grossman's funeral home for Monday morning.

On Sunday night, Ira woke up. The dimethyltryptamine had induced a trance and rendered his heartbeat undetectable. Ira woke up just as Lev Grossman began pumping formaldehyde into his arm. Luckily, there was no lasting damage. Ira reported that his arm was asleep, but he otherwise felt quite refreshed. Moreover, the tea was excellent, he said, and would almost certainly go well with Mandel bread.

When Lev Grossman called Nos's mother, Ina, with the news, she was both overjoyed and horrified. She was thrilled, of course, that Lev had survived, but appalled when Lev Grossman told her that the coffin couldn't be returned. So that it shouldn't go to waste, Ina Rabinowitz resolved to use it as a bed for her son. He was outgrowing his crib anyway and, besides, what could be more comfortable than a coffin? Menachem took to it immediately. The sensation of being surrounded by walls on all sides recreated the crib's security. As he grew older, he decorated the coffin with pictures of his favorite baseball players and movie stars. By the time he was a teenager he couldn't imagine sleeping anyplace else.

How fortuitous that he should grow up to become a vampire!

Vampire he was. N. A. Rabinowitz, demon denizen of Brighton Beach. On the mailbox he used the initials. Nosferatu was a terrible name, really. At the time of his becoming, he didn't give the matter much thought. He remembered the name from the F.W. Murnau film, and so took it as his own. It was unfortunate that he didn't consider the issue more carefully because, given his heritage, Nosferatu was just too easy a name to ridicule. Nose-feratu. Nose-far-a-jew. Nose-for-a-jew. The possibilities were endless, and, over the decades, Nos had heard them all from his colleagues. He thought the name was to blame for his being shunned by the vampire community. Nos had considered changing his name back, but whoever heard of a vampire named Menachem? He'd never be taken seriously that way, and if there was one thing Nosferatu Rabinowitz demanded, it was to be taken seriously. This was his right as an immortal creature of the evening. This caller, by his repeated intrusions, had failed to take him seriously, and, so, Nos would take care of them.

Right after he peed.

He simply couldn't tolerate coffee. It went right through him, especially the cold stuff. As Nos relieved himself in the bathroom, he found himself thinking back to the day of his Becoming. He was so young then. When Harriet Gottlieb, the love of his life, made him the offer he couldn't refuse, on the docks of Sheepshead Bay, everything seemed possible. No one had presented him the fine print. Had he known he'd be spending eternity as a middle-aged Jew, would he have made the same choice? Nos rarely engaged in this sort of self-reflection. Apparently, his birthday was a bigger deal than he admitted. He wondered why it should mean anything at all, given his immortality.

The doorbell rang again. This was utterly intolerable! He thought, "Who dares to intrude upon my sanctum, not once, not twice, but thrice?" He would put an end to this, once and for all. Nos zipped his fly, washed his hands as his mother had taught him, and stormed off toward the door resolved to exact a bitter and painful revenge against this intruder. Open here he flung the door to his condominium to find a young girl selling Girl Scout Cookies.

"I'm Rachel," she said. "Would you like to support my troop?" Rachel had green eyes, brown hair tied in a pigtail, and was so slight of frame that she could barely hold up her uniform. She reminded Nos faintly of Harriet Gottlieb, and he found himself drifting again into the past, to the summer of his love. But then he noticed the Star of David around Rachel's neck, and, in a flash, she had his full attention. Dinner.

"Are you Jewish?" he asked.

"Yes," she said.

"Then come in, come in. I'll get some money."

The thought of eating a nine-year-old girl appalled Nos, but he was desperate. He didn't like the idea of eating a little girl, but one must appreciate the difficulties of life as a Jewish vampire. To be kosher, Jewish law requires that an animal both have cloven hooves and regurgitate its food. They must be killed swiftly, with a single knife stroke across the throat. These edicts presented some obvious challenges for Nos. Many people in New York City regurgitate their food, but very few have cloven hooves. To make matters worse, the Torah forbids the consumption of animal blood.

Desperate, Nos sought an audience with the preeminent rabbinical scholar, Moishe Feinstein. While Rebbe Feinstein tried on a new pair of Hush Puppies at Kings Plaza, Nos explained his situation.

"This is quite a predicament," said the Rabbi. "On the one hand, we must obey kosher law to be a good Jew. But, on the hand, does not the Talmud also teach us that orthodoxy must be balanced against a person's well-being and happiness? Even on Yom Kippur, the Holiest of Holies, are not children and the sick allowed to eat?"

"Yes, rabbi. This is my dilemma."

"I'll take the shoes," the Rabbi said. "They are very comfortable, and does not the Torah teach us that the feet are at the bottom of the body?"

Then, to Nos, he said, "For you, we must make a compromise. God does not want you to starve. Look at you, for God's sake, you're all skin and bones. Here is my ruling. You may consume human flesh and blood, but only the flesh and blood of Jews. Anything else will be considered *tref*."

"Yes, Rabbi."

"To simulate the rules for slaughter, you must wear a dental dam around your fangs."

"Yes, Rabbi."

"And killing is never allowed on Shabbat, unless it is a telemarketer, in which case it is encouraged."

"Yes, Rabbi."

Elated, Nos glided away from the mall. He'd been prepared for worse. Rabbi Feinstein had offered a brilliant and generous interpretation of conflicting scripture. Nos did know whether to attribute his good fortune to an exercise of Solomonic wisdom or to the good feelings the Hush Puppies had given the Rabbi, whose feet were notoriously difficult to fit.

Even with Feinstein's blessing, though, Nos couldn't bring himself to kill anyone. He wasn't assertive by nature. At Yeshiva, Pincus Sinatra, the singer's illegitimate son, stole Menachem's *tzedakah* money twenty-seven weeks in a row. In games of *Diplomacy*, he was always Luxembourg. It was nearly a year after his meeting with Rabbi Feinstein before Nos made his first killing, a middle-aged Hasidic perfumer, and that was only because he wouldn't stop *schvtzing* him in the mall. Three times the man asked if he wanted to try the cologne. Three times

Nosferatu said no. And still he sprayed him with the cologne! In a fit of rage, Nos killed the man, but he regretted it almost immediately. It was a terrible meal. The smell was awful, and Nos picked *payis* from his teeth for weeks.

For a while, he subsisted on hot dogs and Jägermeister, which he'd been told contained traces of deer blood. This wasn't a long-term solution. After a few months of this diet, Nos developed a nervous tic and an explosive case of diarrhea. Thereafter, he subsisted mostly on laboratory mice, which he purchased with his meager earnings from the night shift he worked at the *7-Eleven*. He got almost no protein. He couldn't even eat peanut butter because of his diverticulitis. Snakes ate better.

This was no way for a vampire to live!

For his birthday, Nos resolved to become more assertive. As his first step, he went to the bookstore, just after New Year's Day, and bought Roger Dawon's *Thirteen Secrets of Power Performance*. For the past six months, Nos had been focused on implementing one: Take What You Want! Now, standing before him in a size-seven plaid skirt, was his great test. How fortuitous that it should come on his sixtieth birthday!

Nos feared that Rachel had been taught to fear strangers, but she was a trusting girl, and Nos had a trustworthy face. As she stepped inside his studio apartment, Nos became intoxicated with desire. It had been so long since he had eaten properly. Naturally he began to think about desert.

"What type of cookies do you have there?" he asked. As Rachel leaned over to peer into her bag, she exposed her neck to Nos. It was smooth and tender. It couldn't have been more different than the neck of the Hasidic perfumer. Finally, he would eat well. As she rummaged, he leaned in to feast.

Wait! Had he washed his hands after he went to the bathroom? His mother taught him always to wash his hands before he ate. He replayed the moment in his mind, but he couldn't be sure. He'd been distracted thinking about his birthday when the doorbell rang. Nos shuddered. It would be repulsive to eat dinner after having gone to the bathroom without washing his hands. But there was no time. He couldn't very well ask Rachel to wait for him to bite her neck while he went to the bathroom to wash his hands.

Here was another dilemma of Talmudic proportions! On the one hand, Take What You Want! One the other, Wash Your Hands! What would Roger Dawson say? Nos doubted that even Moishe Feinstein could help if he were still alive, may he rest in peace. Besides, Young Rachel was no more likely to wait around while he sought the counsel of a rabbi than she was to wait for him to wash his hands. She'd surely run off. Who was he kidding anyway? If this was a day to tell truths, he might as well tell himself the biggest truth of all: he wasn't cut out to be a vampire.

Rachel looked up from her boxes. "I have Thin Mints and Tagg-a-longs."

Nos didn't know what Tagg-a-longs were, but he was embarrassed to ask. On the other hand, he knew he didn't like mints.

"I'll take two boxes of the Tagg-a-longs," he said.

Rachel handed him the cookies. He handed her ten

dollars.

"Thank you for supporting my troop," she said.

"You're welcome."

Nos closed the door and went back into his house. Ten dollars seemed like a lot of money for two boxes of cookies, but he'd have been embarrassed to ask for change. Out of curiosity, he went to the bathroom, and saw from the water in the sink that he had indeed washed his hands.

"C'est la vie," he said to himself, and, with a shrug of his shoulders, opened the Tagg-a-longs, pulled one out, and took a bite.

Peanut butter.

Risk Takers

On a cold January evening, shortly after the first substantial snowfall of the season, August Willard reassumed his role as Supreme Commandant of the United Advanced Global Forces (Expeditionary). He donned his hat, gloves, tartan winter coat, popped into the living room, and planted a kiss on the cheek of his wife, who was watching television. Without looking up from *Project Accessory*, she said, "Put on your galoshes."

August hated galoshes, but he didn't protest. If, for example, he told her that his shoes were waterproof and would suffice, she'd remind him of his susceptibility to colds and his bout with pneumonia eleven years earlier, which began with wet feet. Undoubtedly, she'd add that he couldn't afford to be sick because his inadequate job offered inadequate health insurance. This would pen August into a corner from which, based on his tactical experience, he wouldn't be able to extricate himself.

Other avenues were equally fraught. If he said that galoshes made him feel poor, which they did, he'd avoid having to defend the low ground of his less than robust health, but would be forced into a more direct conflagration regarding his career choices. On this subject August had viable defenses. He'd chosen to remain at Our Lady St. Mary Catherine of the Ascension because he enjoyed the students and because shifting to a public school, the course of action Ginny Willard favored for its higher salary and superior benefits, would have involved a substantial measure of uncertainty. In the court of public opinion, August might even have prevailed in this exchange, but in the court of family opinion, the position was hopeless. Like most Catholic schools, Our Lady St. Mary Catherine didn't grant tenure. Ginny Willard asked, not unreasonably, how much worse off her husband could be in the city system? At this point, August could say that no public school would hire a 62-year-old Americanist, but Ginny had been making the same argument for 35 years, and believed that August shouldn't benefit rhetorically from his own inordinate delay.

Alternatively, August could tell Ginny that galoshes

reminded him of his mother, who'd never bought big enough rubbers, and so little Auggie spent hours prying them on or off, his mother hovering over his shoulder, chiding him that he wasn't using the plastic bags effectively, that he should place them over the shoe not inside the galosh, or inside the galosh not over the shoe, until finally one day a teenaged August screamed at her, "The plastic bags do nothing!" irrevocably altering their relationship. August knew that the mere invocation of his mother's name would escalate the conflict, and so, with no good option available to him, he said nothing.

August regarded this capacity for forbearance as essential to his tactical virtuosity. In the chess game of life, he could see several turns ahead. He could see all the possible moves, all of the responses to these potential moves, the responses to the responses, the sur-sur-responses, and dispassionately determine the best course of action. Under certain circumstances this meant refraining from action. This capacity was rare. Few generals could withstand the human impulse to act. How different might history have been if Osami

Nagano had prevailed over Isoroku Yamamoto and restrained the Japanese Combined Fleet from attacking Hawaii or if Hitler had refrained from opening the Eastern front?

August sat on the foyer bench and pried on the galoshes. He groaned loudly several times to ensure his wife knew that he'd complied with her wishes, then closed the door behind him. The temperatures had been mild throughout the past several days—ideal for snow production—and now that the winds had subsided it felt almost pleasant outside, but the snow was out of control. The first flakes had fallen more than two days earlier, but Richmond Hill residents still hadn't seen a single plow. Ginny reported some speculation at church that the sanitation workers were staging a wildcat strike, but August doubted they'd get much sympathy. Times were tough all across the country. Mostly, though, he worried how he'd extract his car from a 14-inch snowdrift. Generally speaking, he concerned himself only with matters within his control. This was another facet of his tactical expertise.

By the time August reached the end of his block—the corner of 119th and Bessemer, he knew he'd be late. More than half the homeowners had failed to shovel their sidewalks and he found himself wading through snowdrifts. The galoshes were useless. The snow was substantially deeper than the galoshes were tall, so when he stepped into an accumulation, snow seeped into his rubbers where it melted and pooled. Each time he took a step he experienced an unpleasant squishing, and thought of Ginny.

Ordinarily, he walked to Phil's through Forest Park, but this wouldn't be possible, so instead of continuing on Bessmer, he made a right on 118th Street, and crossed town on Metropolitan Avenue. Without traffic, it seemed eerily quiet. To his left, the park, blanketed in virgin snow, beckoned to August. He would've liked nothing more than to lose himself there, amidst the ancient oaks, but wars didn't take off for blizzards.

On the far side of the park, August turned right on Puritan, left on Greenway, and knocked on Phil Yarnow's place. He was almost 20 minutes late, and had an apology prepared, but Phil lifted the burden from his shoulders when he opened the door. "I'm so glad you made it, Auggie," he said. "I didn't think you'd come, but I called Ginny and she said you were on the way."

Of course, August would've crossed Forest Park in a nuclear holocaust, as Phil would have, but they maintained a superficial nonchalance about their engagement. This veneer helped smooth things over back in the day when August and Ginny dined with the Yarnows and at high school reunions. Privately, though, August maintained no delusions about the nature of their relationship, and he knew Phil didn't either. August barely had his galoshes off when Phil said, "Shall we get going?"

Together, they trudged in silence to the battle site. August used the walk downstairs to focus himself. Inevitably, he'd experience one or several moments of envy on his walk to Phil's house. Sometimes these occurred upon entering Forest Hills Gardens with its faux gates, winding streets, and stately oaks, planted by Frederick Law Olmsted's son. Sometimes they occurred upon seeing the Yarnow's six-bedroom Tudor home. Most commonly, though, began when he entered their living room, which had been tastefully furnished from Bloomingdales. Nothing reminded August of his failings quite so powerfully as the "Peninsula" sectional, which retailed for almost $12,000. He and Ginny still employed the living room set bequeathed to them by his mother, whom Ginny despised even in death, and August had to admit, though the couch and sofa had been covered in plastic for the entire tenure of their service to his mother, still smelled faintly of ham.

Phil Yarnow had outdone him in every way, but a basement was just a basement—albeit one with a wet bar, plush carpeting and a back-up living room set superior to his inherited jalopies. But it was still underground—Phil Yarnow hadn't figured a way to buy himself out of that. August reminded himself that the gods of war paid no heed to the choices a general had made since elementary school. They didn't care who went to law school and who'd become a teacher. They didn't care who married their high school sweetheart and who'd married the former Miss New York. They cared only about tactics, strategy and valor.

Downstairs, August's thoughts turned to the war. The war was always on his mind, of course, but the basement inevitably brought things into clearer focus. In his mind, he replayed the hostilities' history. The war's earliest days had been dominated by Freddie Duffy, a pimply-faced delinquent who compensated for his lack of tactical expertise with good luck—he was dealt the entirety of North America, with the exception of Quebec, and extraordinary dice rolling. Had Freddie pursued even a moderately conservative strategy, he surely would have prevailed, but he had an appetite for territory worthy of Genghis Khan. Even still he almost won. In the second hour of combat, he defeated Cal Berry, who really hadn't wanted to play anyway and, three hours later, Sig Ludden, whom he routed with an ill-advised dash through Asia, which could only be understood as an act of spite relating to the senior prom. He even came within a whisker of eliminating Auggie, who made a valiant stand in the Greenland tundra—still his finest hour.

Recklessness could only prevail for so long, though, and the more experienced generals punished Freddie for overextending himself. Phil, who'd spent the early part of the war holed up in Western Australia, crept eastward and northward, until he had control of Australasia and a secure outpost in Siam. In the West, Auggie and the formidable Spector Dylan raced to finish off Freddie. When Auggie prevailed in the pivotal Battle of Brazil, he captured Freddie's reserves, and crippled Spector, who fell soon thereafter, shortly before leaving for Princeton.

Soon, Auggie had control over the Americas. Phil meanwhile gradually expanded northward until he'd claimed the entirety of Asia. Europe and Africa became the primary points of conflict. August and Phil jousted back and forth, attempting to gain control, until each general wordlessly shifted his focus. August began to send more of his resources to the north, while Phil's went south, eventually leading Auggie to acquire Europe while Asia went to Phil. For a while there would be occasional flare-ups—most commonly between East Africa and the Middle East, which were each notoriously difficult to defend. Over time, though, these conflagrations became increasingly rare, as Phil and August dedicated more resources to reinforcing their borders. Sometimes Phil would launch a token attack, so that he could collect his allocation of armies, or vice-versa, but soon even these minor skirmishes subsided. The western hemisphere was a sea of blue; red controlled the east. This picture had remained essentially unchanged for 39 years.

"It's your turn," Phil said, as soon as the men sat down. Phil used to offer Auggie a drink or put out some nuts, but Auggie would always refuse the beverage, lest he require the bathroom and show weakness, and he never snacked during combat, especially on something salted. Now they simply got down to business.

Though August had thought about his move all week, he reviewed his thought process. He regarded this as another of his virtues. Most generals would settle on a course of action and implement it without further thought. Auggie, by contrast, always reconsidered the entire situation before acting. It was essential to do this over the board, to process all new information. Of course, there hadn't been any new information since the early-1970s, but Auggie double-checked himself, nevertheless.

North Africa remained, as it had for decades, the most tempting point of attack. Auggie thought Phil had made a strategic blunder in allocating his troops. He had 2,700 armies in North Africa, and approximately 1,400 in his other exposed fronts in Egypt Ural, Afghanistan, the Middle East, and Kamchatka. But the latter four countries were only exposed on one front each, as opposed to North Africa, which faced attack from Western and Southern Europe and Brazil, which was connected via land bridge. Combined, Auggie had more than 3,500 armies on these three counties.

A less experienced general might have succumbed to the temptation, but August knew better. Military commanders, like slot jockeys, tended only to see upside. Sure, Napoleon *could have* successfully invaded Russia while simultaneously attacking the Iberian Peninsula. He barely considered, though, how much failure would weaken the Grande Armée.

August faced a similar dilemma to Napoleon's. Computer simulations estimated his chance of prevailing in North Africa at 50.73%. This, of course, meant the chance of failure was 49.27%. If he indeed failed, August would be vulnerable to retaliatory counter-attacks. Phil would have an easy time sweeping through Europe with his Egyptian forces. August would have a reasonable prospect of recapturing Europe with his Ukrainian reserves, but this would leave him weakened in the eastern theatre and vulnerable to attack from Ural and Afghanistan. According to further simulations, he'd have between a 30 and 40 percent chance of withstanding this counter-offensive, depending how well or poorly the earlier campaigns went. If he managed to survive, though, his forces would be decimated. Eurasia's fate would be a matter of chance. To a commander of August's statute, this was intolerable.

August could initiate an attack and see how things went, but any failure would create the perception of vulnerability. This was the nub of the rub. Schlieffen and Hitler's real failures had been to allow the Allies to believe they could prevail. Same with Napoleon. In August's view, the usefulness of a veneer of invincibility couldn't be overstated. If he attacked North Africa and failed, Phil would feel momentum. He'd smell blood. This possibility of lending comfort to the enemy led August to conclude that the attack couldn't be justified. He reviewed his thinking a final time and announced his decision.

"I pass," he said.

This moved the ball into Phil's court. Like any good chess player, August attempted to view the situation from his opponent's perspective. Phil had displayed conservative tendencies throughout the contest. Holing up in Australasia was a reasonable strategy, but Phil had persisted too long in his isolationism. He'd refrained from attacking Sig Ludden when he was weak, and he made no attempt to take out Spector Dylan when he had the chance. By contrast, when August perceived the opportunity to vanquish Spector, he moved swiftly and aggressively. August regarded decisiveness as his greatest strength as a commander. Phil's lack of conviction was an Achilles heel.

In August's view, Phil should have perceived an opportunity. Ukraine, like North Africa, could be attacked on three fronts. Simulations showed that a simultaneous attack from Ural, the Middle East, and Afghanistan had a 51.06% chance of success. Phil would have run the same simulations, but August knew that he'd never pull the trigger. If his offensive failed, Phil would be susceptible to counter-attack from August's southern European forces. Given how exposed Phil had left his rear flank, August might drive all the way to Australia. Phil would only see the risks, not the bold path to victory. Phil could launch an exploratory attack and see how things went, but he'd be daunted by the psychological consequences of a loss.

This was an essential difference between the two generals. August never thought about how a loss would impact him. This possibility he regarded with utter dispassion, as all great generals must. He worried solely about the positive effect it would have on Phil. Phil, on the other hand, anticipated his own sulking brood. In August's view, this exemplified the essential difference between the two generals. Auggie acted with Vulcan-like dispassion. Phil, on the other hand, allowed his feelings to get the best of him. He experienced fear, an emotion no great general could indulge.

After approximately 30 minutes, Phil announced his move. "I pass," he said. August knew better than to reveal himself to his adversary, but inwardly he smiled with satisfaction. *Just as I expected*, he thought to himself.

On his turn, August took a fresh look at the board. He'd meticulously trained himself to consider all new information. No pieces had moved, but Phil's pass gave further invaluable insight into his psychology. August reviewed his possible attacks, and potential counterattacks, and phlegmatically reached his decision.

"I pass," he announced.

True to form, Phil passed 15 minutes later. After careful

analysis, August followed suit, and soon thereafter, Phil passed again. On his fourth turn, August conceived an entirely new scenario: he could redeploy his Ukrainian forces in Alaska. The reallocation, which would take several years since only two armies could be moved at a time, would place additional pressure on Kamchatka. On the other hand, it would leave August more exposed in Europe. Furthermore, Phil could move his western Asian forces to Kamchatka more rapidly than August could get his troops to Alaska. August regarded this capacity to dispassionately assess even his own ideas as an even greater strength than his capacity to brainstorm new ones. After ruminating for 40 minutes, August rejected the new scenario.

"I pass," he said.

Following ten minutes of intense concentration, Phil announced, "I pass."

At precisely eleven o'clock, while August was considering his next move, Phil said, "time." By mutual agreement, they played from precisely seven o'clock until eleven o'clock, each

Sunday evening, except holidays. Years ago, Phil sometimes would offer August a drink upon the temporary cessation of hostilities, but August couldn't imagine socializing so shortly after being in the heat of battle, and inevitably declined.

"I'll get your coat," Phil said.

"Thanks."

"Don't forget your galoshes."

"Right."

Upstairs, near the coat tree, Phil held open the front door. "Say hi to Ginny."

"And to Ina." Ina used to come downstairs to greet August, or to say goodbye, but that hadn't happened in 30 years. August found it difficult to make small talk when the war was on his mind. The couples' dinners had ended for essentially the same reason.

"See you next week," Phil said.

"See you next week."

The roads had only gotten worse, and August made slow progress home. He didn't mind, though. The conditions and late hour deterred even the bravest driver, and so he had Metropolitan Avenue to himself. He imagined what the city must have been like, once upon a simpler time. In Forest Park, fresh icicles dangled from the oak trees, and the grove beckoned to him. August thought again how magical it would be to lose himself in there for a while, wandering the snow-covered paths. He wouldn't mind avoiding his wife's disapproval for another hour or two.

But August understood the risks involved, too. He could slip and fall, and if by chance he broke an ankle, it might be months before someone discovered him in the backwoods. It was easy to imagine someone dying of exposure, and the harsh judgment that would fall upon him for having wandered in the snow into the recess of a park, which was underutilized on the nicest of days. August weighed the potential happiness he'd enjoy against the harm he'd cause his wife and society in general. Dispassionately, he concluded that his pleasure would be fleeting, and accordingly should be discounted. August regarded this ability to view his pleasure and pain as counting no more or less than anyone else's as another of his great strengths as a general and a human being. He looked at the park one more time, then bravely continued on his way home—the silence interrupted only by the sound of his squishing galoshes, as he thought to himself, "War is hell."

<u>The (Revised) Protocols of the Elders of Zion</u>

I was lounging on my couch one evening, watching Harry Connick Jr. take someone down on *American Idol*, when a telemarketer called and asked me whether I might be interested in joining the Elders of Zion. Of course, she didn't ask me this straight away. She first asked how I was doing and whether I was enjoying my evening and other banalities that I ignored because I was too busy remonstrating myself for having answered the phone and wondering whether I could hang up without being impolite. When the pleasantries concluded, she asked, "Would you be interested in taking out a subscription to *The Nation?*"

"I already have one," I said. *Of course.*

"In that case," she asked, "would you be interested in joining an elite organization of Jews that controls all of the world's major financial markets and governments?"

I considered this question for a moment. Like everyone else, I'd heard whispers about the existence of the Elders of Zion. But I'd heard whispers, too, about the Illuminati and the creation of a New World Order. And I'd read about the pervasive influence of Masons and sinister black helicopters. I presumed that each of these were hoaxes, or kernels of facts surrounded by so much revision and exaggeration as to be unrecognizable from the truth. How exciting that one of these conspiracy theories should turn out to be true! And in favor of my side!

"Sure," I told the woman on the phone. "Who wouldn't be interested in joining an elite organization of Jews that controls all of the world's major financial markets and governments?"

"Fine," she said. "Someone will be in touch with you shortly."

Straight away, I called my mother. I've always been a bit of a disappointment to her. She had her heart set on a doctor, not a wannabe stand-up comedian who worked the check-out counter at Whole Foods. I thought this might be just the thing to turn around her opinion of me and brighten her day.

"Hi, Mom," I said.

"Hi, son."

"I've been asked to join the Elders of Zion!"

"That's very nice. So, what is the Elders of Zion?"

"It is an elite organization of Jews that controls all of the world's major financial markets and governments. You can tell all your friends at Mahjongg!"

"Does this mean that you'll be going to medical school?"

"I don't think so, mom."

"Then I won't tell the girls at Mahjongg. How are things at the supermarket?"

"I've told you, it's not a supermarket. It's a Whole Foods."

"Do they sell eggs and laundry detergent?"

"Yes."

"Do they have long lines and cashiers?"

"Yes."

"Then it's a supermarket."

Clearly I was never going to win this one. My mother couldn't bring me down, though. I glided through the next several days. My feet barely touched the ground, as I walked back and forth to work, and puttered around my apartment, waiting to be contacted. When the invitation arrived, it tempered my enthusiasm slightly. The meeting would be held at the Raleigh. I'd never cared for the Catskills. As a child, my parents always took my brothers and me there for vacation. Our family ran the gamut of hotels, from Grossinger's to the Nevele. To me they were all the same, and every day the same. We'd sit by the pool, with occasional breaks for shuffleboard, kishka and Borscht. In the evenings, we'd watch Henny Youngman or Irwin Corey, if we out of luck, and, finally, participate in an insufferable group activity. I saw more Mambo Nights than anyone ever should.

But as I made the familiar drive west on Route 17, I could scarcely contain my excitement. My mind raced with possibilities, thinking about the potential good that an organization with so much influence could accomplish. I felt almost dizzy. This enthusiasm dampened only slightly when the person outside the conference room asked me for an initiation fee of $100.

"To whom shall I make out the check?" I asked.

"Cash," he replied.

"I'd prefer to make it out in the name of the organization, so I have a record for tax purposes."

"With the exception of the National Organization of Women, no group with aims of world domination has succeeded in securing non-profit status."

"What about American Express? That way I can get frequent flier miles."

"We only take Diners Club."

I sighed, and handed over the cash, but when I entered the conference room my momentary disgruntlement evaporated. Never before had I seen a sight so wondrous as this. All of the members of the Jewish cabal gathered in a single place. And such a collection of wisdom and talent! Overcoming my sense of intimation, I walked around the room and introduced myself to each of the Elders. To Jerry Seinfeld, I said, "I'm so pleased to meet you. I am such a fan."

"What's the deal with all of these fans?" he asked. "Why don't people get air conditioning? The fan is so nineteenth century."

I laughed.

To Al Franken, I said, "I just sent you my money."

"Thank you," he replied, deadpanned as always.

To Howard Stern I said, "Baba Booey."

"Megadildoes," he replied.

To Don Rickles I said, "It's such an honor."

"You look like a turnip with glasses," he answered.

I nearly fell over myself walking around that table, fawning over one genius after another.

"I'm your biggest fan," I told Woody Allen.

"That's not possible," he said, his arms flailing. "There's an obese diabetic in Scranton who loved *Bananas*."

"That's a handsome undershirt," I told Freddie Roman.

"You look great," I said to Joan Rivers. "Have you had work?"

When I finally found my seat in front of a paper plate

adorned with a scoop of chopped liver and a sliver of carrot, I couldn't believe my luck. As I drank the can of White Rock cola that had been set in front of me, I felt intoxicated with power.

Lorne Michaels called the meeting to order. "As everybody knows, things have not been going well," he said. "Jewish popularity is at an all-time low. Ever since *Seinfeld* went off the air our numbers have been plummeting—and our numbers weren't all that good to begin with. The problem is the economy. Unemployment is up to six percent. Manufacturing has been especially hard hit. The trade deficit is nearly half a trillion dollars. Not surprisingly, half of Americans think the economy is heading in the wrong direction. Needless to say, we get the blame." Michaels paused. He possessed substantial gravitas. Even in such an august room, he commanded everyone's attention. "The good news is that I think we have an answer. I'll let Joe Franklin explain."

Few people have the confidence and stature to follow Lorne Michaels, but Joe Franklin surely did. When he finished clearing his throat, the Elders hung on his every word. "My friends, nothing promotes confidence in our people so much as confidence in the economy. And nothing promotes confidence in the economy so much as home ownership. Yet, for years, mortgages have been closed to potential homeowners with credit scores below 640. As a result, nearly forty percent of Americans households are forced to rent their residences. In the African-American and Hispanic-American communities, homeownership rates are less than fifty percent. I'm here today to propose that we relax credit standards."

"This is the motion," said Lorne Michaels.

Joe Franklin passed around some charts laying out the details of his proposal. Even to my untrained eye, the benefits were clear. By relaxing standards to a 600 credit score, homeownership rates would increase by nearly ten percent. In the Hispanic-American community the gain would be as much as twenty percent.

Mel Brooks raised his hand and Lorne Michaels recognized him. "Obvious question, guys, but what happens if these new homeowners can't afford to make their mortgage payments?"

Lorne Michaels smiled. "Here's the beautiful thing."

Joe Franklin picked up the thread. "If they can't make the payments, then they'll just refinance their mortgage. The lower we set the standards, the more people are eligible for all kinds of credit—that means not just purchase mortgages, but refinance money too."

"And what if they can't meet those payments?"

"Then they'll refinance again," Franklin said. "The beauty is that we can always lower credit standards further. This creates a virtuous cycle, opening up homeownership to more and more people."

"It's brilliant," said Jerry Stiller.

"Genius," said Jon Stewart.

"Why restrict it to people with credit scores of higher than 600? Why not make it available to all but the provenly unreliable?"

Several cried "yes, yes," and Lewis Black proclaimed in his familiar indignant tone, "Homeownership should be a right, not a privilege."

"I take that as a friendly amendment," Franklin said, smiling.

"Do we have a consensus?" Michaels asked.

It appeared so by nods and smiles and general positive energy, with the notable exception of a bespectacled man, bald but for some crazy, curly tufts projecting from the side of his head, and oddly dressed in a t-shirt and sports jacket. This curmudgeon raised his hand in a manner that made clear that he objected, not just to this, but to life itself.

Michaels acknowledged him. "Larry."

"This presumes that housing prices will keep going up."

Jackie Mason chimed in. "Larry, housing prices in the United States have been rising steadily for more than a century."

"But what if they don't?"

Gilbert Gottfried said, "The sky could fall tomorrow, too. Who know what happens then either?"

"I'm serious. What's the plan?"

This fellow just wouldn't back down. "Who is this guy?" I whispered to my neighbor, Alan King.

"Larry David," he answered. "He was a producer on *Seinfeld*. He rode Jerry's coattails to the tune of half a billion dollars."

"Jesus," I said.

"We try not to say that here."

Meanwhile, Joe Franklin attempted to respond to Larry David's question. "Even if we witnessed a short-term drop in housing prices, other borrowers would simply step in and suck up the available stock. Opportunistic buyers would have a field day."

"Of course, that presumes that credit remains liquid."

This comment broke everyone up. Albert Brooks fell out of his chair. Sid Caesar laughed so hard I thought he'd split his pants. Buddy Hackett could barely breathe. As he struggled to compose himself, in between gasps, Hackett cried, "And I suppose that you think the shadow banking system will collapse too."

"Any other ideas, Larry?" asked Richard Lewis, tears coming from his eyes.

Harold Ramis howled, "Maybe you want to revive your idea for a sit-com about a misanthropic middle-aged Jew?"

The hilarity continued for almost a minute, during which I noticed that this Larry David seemed shockingly unbothered by the ridicule. When the laughter finally subsided, Lorne Michaels asked, "Is there anything else?" No one raised a hand, so he said, "Let's take a vote." I felt proud to cast my ballot for a measure that would have such a positive impact on the American economic system and, by extension the reputation of my people. The final tally was thirty-seven-to-one with Larry David casting the only dissenting vote.

When the meeting adjourned, shortly thereafter, they put out Hamentaschen and decaf, and the already good mood became jubilant. People congratulated themselves on what they'd accomplished, laughed about Larry David's obstreperousness, and when the time soon came to leave, bid each other farewell until the next session. It all seemed great, though one thing had been troubling me. On the way out of the conference room, I button-holed Alan King, who'd shared his pickle tray with me at lunch, and seemed generally approachable.

"Mr. King," I said. "May I ask you a question?"

"Shoot kid."

"How long have Jews controlled the world's major banks and governments?"

"For pretty much as long as our people have been around. Nearly six thousand years, kid."

"Well, Mr. King, why is it then that Jews have had such a hard time of it throughout history—you know with the Inquisition and the Holocaust and all of the anti-Semitism?"

"It's the killing Jesus thing, kid."

"But that's a vicious rumor spread to vilify Jews."

"Nah, it's true. In the year 30, a Spanish boy took a

message to Fyvush Flavius, who was the head of the Elders of Zion at the time. 'Pontius Pilate is about to kill Jesus,' he said. Trouble is he used the Spanish pronunciation. As fate had it, Fyvush Flavius had ordered takeaway Chinese from Wok Maximus the night before, and the delivery boy, whose name was Jesus, had forgotten the duck sauce. So, when Flavius heard that Jesus was about to be crucified, he said, 'Let him die.' The rest, as they say, is history."

As we stepped outside, we handed out tickets to the valet, and Alan King put his arm around my shoulder. "But today changes everything. It's a new day now, kid. A new day."

We bid one another farewell, and I watched King drive away into the sunset. When the valet delivered my Toyota Tercel, I handed him a quarter, and drove off myself. In the bright sunshine of that summer day, I saw the ancient mountains in a way I never had before. The Earth seemed new, reborn.

"It's a new day," I said to myself. "A new day."

Alma Mater, Alma Pater

The first thing Ben Brogan noticed at his reunion was how much smaller his high school was in real life than his memories. Ben had experienced this effect before with other scenes from his childhood—the par-three golf course behind his grandmother's Florida condominium, the knish store across from his other grandmother's apartment in Brighton Beach, the Nathan's in Coney Island, but none of these disparities approached the magnitude of this one. In his mind's eye, Levittown High School was an endless labyrinthine expanse of hallways and classrooms and offices, as if the Pentagon had been occupied by volatile hormone-soaked teenagers and a handful of defeated teachers, counting the days until their pensions kicked in. In real life, it looked like a dreary pipsqueak of a building better suited to serve the mentally ill than aspiring-to-college teenagers, which might have been the point.

The second thing Ben Brogan noticed at his reunion was the music. Since his and his classmates' graduation, twenty-five years ago, music had undergone a revolution. Grunge had come and gone, U2 had reinvented itself five times, Green Day went from the Gilman to the St. James Theatre. Bruce Springsteen and Bono proved that mainstream musicians could display a social conscience. The Black Keys, Arcade Fire, and dozens of other bands pushed envelopes and defied genre labels. In spite of that history, the loudspeakers played Debbie Gibson's "Foolish Beat." None of his classmates appeared to be wearing their clothes from 1988, no one showed up in the same car, no one, he presumed, would spend any time discussing what had gone wrong with the Dukakis campaign. Yet, they apparently felt compelled to listen to the same music they'd listened to in his school. If the organizers had wanted to maintain a connection to their youth, they could have chosen an artist from the era who remained relevant, such as Neil Young, or a band that continued to tour, like the Rolling Stones, or, if they felt compelled to stick with a quintessentially 80's artist, at least one that was halfway decent. A-ha or the Cars wouldn't have offended him. The choice of Debbie Gibson stupefied Ben.

The third thing Ben Brogan noticed at his reunion was Chris Schiller. Chris was four persons ahead of Ben in the check-in queue. Ben saw Chris before Chris saw him, and Ben shifted his position in the line so that the person in front of him on line would block Chris's view. The maneuver worked. Chris registered and entered the gymnasium without noticing him. Nevertheless, Ben's heart sunk. Seeing Chris, his principal antagonist from high school, brought back a flood of negative emotions, which, organically speaking, shouldn't have been possible.

Ben's therapist had contended that confronting Chris would be good for Ben. Ben had great respect for his therapist, whom he flew in from New York for their twice-weekly sessions. People could say all the positive things they wanted about northern California psychologists, but in Ben's view, therapists were like pizza and bagels. You couldn't get a decent one outside of New York City. They'd been discussing the reunion for nearly five years. Mendel Gerbler found Ben's preoccupation with the reunion highly significant, and, in Gerbler's view, suggested that Ben had never fully emerged from the latent stage of development. This explained, at least in part, why Ben sublimated so much of his libidinal energy into his work. It explained, too, why he focused externally for approval, and tended to attribute causation for his feelings to others rather than himself. In Gerbler's view, returning to the scene of the crime, as they liked to call it, would help Ben demonstrate his own growth to himself, which should help soothe his perpetually dissatisfied ego. In the simplest terms, Ben had never grown up.

Gerbler's hypothesis regarding his psyche struck Ben as plausible, and, generally speaking had high regard for his doctor, but they parted ways regarding the potential usefulness of attending the reunion. Gerbler's worldview could sometimes be problematic. He was a devoted Freudian, who'd studied at the Anna Freud Institute in London. Ben once asked him whether, at the Freud Institute, twelve-week semesters lasted only ten weeks, but Gerbler didn't get it, or at least didn't allow himself to offer any sign that he got it. For his part, Ben didn't always get the Freudian insights. Sometimes it took Gerbler to interesting places—he was onto something regarding the dynamics of Ben's childhood, but sometimes Gerbler didn't make sense, as was the case with his view that Ben should attend the reunion.

Ben had spent most of his adult life getting far away as he could—geographically, intellectually, and socially—from the Philistines of Long Island. He had repressed, often actively, the overwhelming majority of his high school experiences. The mere thought of returning for his reunion had caused him to break out in hives. Years before a reunion committee had been formed, arrangements made, and invitations printed, Ben had been fretting about the event and wishing that it were already in the past. In his view, whatever small benefits might accrue from suffering through four hours of miniature egg rolls and contrived conversation couldn't justify the stress. But Ben aimed to please Gerbler, a proclivity they had discussed in exquisite detail during the four-day-a-week phase of their relationship, and so he found himself in line, in front of the gymnasium where he'd experienced his first atomic wedgie, waiting to check in for his 25th reunion.

A gaggle of former cheerleaders manned the registration table, and when Ben reached the front of the queue he had the good fortune to be served by Jill Murray, a blonde, perky type, who'd been kind to him in high school, or, more accurately, not substantially unkind, which in Ben's mind equated to substantial kindness. Jill had kept herself thin, retained her perkiness of spirit, if not entirely of body, and all in all, looked pretty good for forty-three. Ben recognized her immediately. On the other hand, Jill understandably didn't recognize Ben.

"Hi! Welcome back to Levittown High!" she said perkily.

"Hi, Jill," he said, with the most perk he could muster, which wasn't very much.

"I'm so sorry. Remind me of your name, please."

"Ben," he said. "Ben Brogan."

"Oh my goodness, Ben!" she exclaimed, as if she were happy to see him, which was inconceivable. "You look wonderful. I'm sorry I didn't recognize you."

Ben admired how carefully Jill treated his feelings, but the plain fact was that Jill couldn't possibly have recognized him, at least not without a DNA test. Since high school, Ben had had his entire face reconstructed including, most notably, his formerly prodigious nose. He'd replaced his hair follicles with a lustrous beaver fiber more to his liking than his natural, stringy brown hair, used an experimental bone grafting procedure to add five inches in height, transplanted new corneas for better vision, new irises for bluer eyes, new titanium-enhanced dentures for better, more durable teeth, enhanced his musculature with a state-of-the-art hormone cocktail, and that was just the exterior. His doctors had implanted inside him a cardio-vascular attaché, which periodically injected his heart with beta-blockers that lowered his pulse rate, reduced inflammation, and helped him maintain a calm disposition. The device also regularly dispatched nano-robots that scrubbed his arteries clean. He also adhered to a strict 700-calorie per day diet, enhanced by injections of vitamins and resveratrol, which, in combination with the other steps, had substantially retarded his aging process. While Jill look good for forty-three, Ben looked good for thirty, and if his classmates could have checked under his hood, they'd have said he looked pretty damned good for twenty, too. On top of all this, Ben wore $5,000 suits, though, in the grander context, this seemed unremarkable.

"What have you been doing?" Jill asked.

"This and that," Ben said, fulfilling his resolution not to boast about his accomplishments.

"Well, you look great," she said.

"You do too," he replied. "I always thought you were beautiful back in high school, and you still are." This wasn't true. Ben had never noticed Jill in high school, nor any other girl for that matter, but admitting a crush seemed like the sort of thing to say at a reunion to someone you wanted to make feel good about herself, and Ben felt that Jill deserved to feel good about herself for being kind to him. His compliment appeared to have the desired effect. His hyper-acute vision detected a subtle dilation of her pupils and a swelling of the capillaries in her cheeks. Then she smiled, which one didn't need enhanced eyesight to detect. Ben smiled in return, and made his way inside with a lighter heart.

The gymnasium had been done up in style, and Ben almost didn't recognize it as the former site of so many indignities. Here he'd been humiliated by his inability to perform a single pull-up, even with the assistance of a chair, or a single push-up, even on his knees. Here, in a white cotton Fruit-of-the-Loom tee-shirt and navy blue gym shorts, held up by a safety pin because he had the waist of a ten-year-old girl, he'd stood for inspection, jutting out his chest to its maximal, still insubstantial circumference, hoping that this year's gym teacher wouldn't comment on his physique, though he always did because this year's gym teacher was always last year's gym teacher. Each September, he, Mr. Durante, would poke him Ben in the chest and proclaim, "Look everyone, the Grand Canyon! Everyone, come get a look at the Grand Canyon!" The students laughed, and then laughed even more when he refused to take a shower

with the rest of the class, although Ben believed, even in
retrospect, that the resulting shame was trivial compared to what
he would have endured had he allowed his classmates to get a
look at his naked sunken chest, which even his relentlessly
optimistic mother, who found the silver lining in everything—
even when her husband left her with a five-year-old son at home,
could find no words for praise other than "smooth." He
furthermore believed, even in retrospect, that his torture at the
hands of Mr. Durante would have been all the more unbearable
had he ever spoken the words on the tip of his tongue, "Look
everyone, the alcoholic gym teacher! Everyone should come get
a look at the alcoholic gym teacher!"

   With the streamers, and the lights, and the waiters in the
white tuxedo jackets, the place looked almost civil. Not
somewhere Ben would ever go of his own volition, needless to
say, but not entirely unpalatable. Ben permitted himself to eat
half a cheese puff, and even enjoyed a couple of brief, cordial
conversations. He spoke with Stu Koren, whom he had sat next
to in advanced placement political science, and who had been a

decent enough guy. After handshakes, Stu said that he hardly recognized Ben, and that he looked great. Stu had gone on to law school, he said, and a partnership at Fried, Frank, which had never been his plan, but with his student loan debt, he didn't have many options starting out after law school, and now he had a wife and kids, and a place in Great Neck, and how could he afford to make a change now? Stu maintained his interest in politics, and they chatted amicably about the upcoming presidential election, Stu boasting that he'd gotten on the Obama bandwagon during the 2004 Senate campaign, before it became a bandwagon, and would serve this time around as a regional fundraising coordinator. Ben confined himself to horse-race assessments, such as "Romney gives the Republicans the best chance" or "Obama needs to distance himself from health care reform," vague claims that never betrayed his true political inclinations, but, in Ben's own view, projected an air of substantial intelligence, precisely what Ben had been shooting for in his fantasies about the reunion.

After Stu left for the punchbowl, Ben slipped into a conversation with Elliot Lent and Nathan Alexander, two fellow geeks who'd been in his computer programming classes. Each said that he hardly recognized Ben, and that he looked wonderful, and after Ben returned the compliments they slipped into a pleasant conversation about their native languages, BASIC, PASCAL and FORTRAN, and marveled about how much had stayed the same in the world of computer programming, even as the universe of computers had undergone the most dramatic revolution.

"Do you remember the Macintoshes in the computer lab?" Elliot asked.

"Heck," said Ben. "I remember our Commodore Pets."

They laughed.

Nathan said, "My iPhone has almost a million times more memory than the Pet."

Elliot said, "Can you imagine how much space it would have taken to do back then what an iPhone does today?"

"A warehouse," Nathan replied. "Although I don't think

they had one big enough to reproduce Siri."

Wistfully, Ben said, "Siri is my best friend."

The men laughed again, and Ben felt very connected. Each worked in the business, Elliot as a medical records programmer, Nathan as a systems consultant, and, in what felt like a safe place, Ben allowed himself to admit that he worked in the software industry in Silicon Valley. At the end of the conversation, after exchanges of business cards, and promises to keep in touch, which would never be kept, Ben thought for a moment that he'd either misremembered high school or that everyone had grown up, including himself. Then Chris Schiller came up to him, slapped him on the back, and said, "Hey, Mr. Bentley."

Mr. Bentley had been of Chris's nicknames for him during high school, and though they'd been long repressed, they all now came flooding back: Einstein, Brainiac, Poindexter, Hal; a series relating to the size of his beak: Toucan Sam, Pinocchio, Nosenstein; another series relating to his 26-inch waist: Bones, the Thin Man, Casper, and the one he despised most of all, the Cambodian; a set relating to unfortunate things he'd said in class: Space Cadet because he said he admired astronauts, Gopher because he said he admired Walter Mondale, Julia Child because he mentioned he liked to cook; and, finally, several names the origin of which he didn't know including, notably, Chris Schiller's favorite, Mr. Bentley. After the wave of dread and nausea subsided, Ben thought of running from the gym, but then he remembered his training and who he was and how disappointing failure would be to Mendel Gerbler. He composed himself and asked, "How'd you recognize me?"

"Piece of cake," Chris said.

"Most people seem to think I look quite different than I did in high school."

"Nah, you haven't changed a bit." Chris said this so affably that it seemed impossible to believe he'd intended any insult, but Ben began to brood. They sat in silence for a few moments, awkwardly since the conversation had only just begun, and Ben stewed until he could help himself no longer, and asked a question that had been on his mind for a quarter century.

"Why did you call me Mr. Bentley?"

"Because you're both gay."

"Mr. Bentley wasn't gay. Paul Frederick, the actor who portrayed him was gay, but the character was not."

"Seems like you know a lot about *The Jeffersons*."

"I'm just saying that the nickname doesn't make any sense."

"I thought Mr. Bentley was gay, so it made sense to me."

"But ultimately, the image is inapt."

"I suppose that depends. Are you gay?" Chris asked.

"I'm not going to deign to answer that question."

"Where do you live?"

"San Francisco."

"Do you have kids?"

"No."

"Are you married?"

"No, but that's a lifestyle choice."

"So, you mean you're gay."

"I am not gay!" Ben shouted, not loud enough to cause a scene, but enough to turn a few heads, and Ben recognized that he'd already come partially undone.

"Jeez, Bentley, you don't have to scream. I'm just trying to make conversation. I don't mean nothing by that."

"You mean you don't mean anything by that."

"You still correcting grammar, Mr. Bentley? You haven't changed one bit."

"No," Ben said. "Empirically speaking, I'm a completely different person."

"I don't understand what that means."

"It means based on evidence and data."

"I know what empirical means. I just don't see how you could use data to prove that someone had changed."

Ben believed one could. In addition to the improvements in his appearance and the function of his cardio-vascular system, Ben's scientists had dramatically transformed his brain. Ben had directed them to gain control over the autonomic nervous system. They'd made enormous strides, and were decades ahead of other researchers. Ben had two of their prototypes inside him—an artificial pineal gland that allowed for conscious regulation of melatonin flow, so Ben could control his daily rhythms, and an implant on his medulla oblongata, which enabled him to regulate his breathing, heart rate, and blood pressure. After the implantation of these devices, Ben noticed the most dramatic change in his disposition. His sleep problems ended, and his disposition, which previously could be nervous and irritable, had become phlegmatic.

A philosopher, whom Ben employed on his staff, considered the situation at great length and concluded that following the surgeries Ben was no longer the same person. Ben, in turn, considered that the philosopher might have offered this opinion thinking it was what Ben wanted to hear. After all, who else would pay an Oxford graduate $300,000 a year to think about questions of identity? But Ben dismissed these fears. He felt like a different person, and if an Oxford Ph.D. said so, who was he to question his judgment? Of course, none of this would make any sense to Chris Schiller.

"You just have to trust me," Ben said. "I'm a new man."

"It doesn't seem that way," Chris said. "You were always stuck on yourself, and a little bit too concerned what people thought about you. Seems to me you haven't changed one bit, Bentley."

They stood in silence again, a prolonged awkward silence, during which Ben stared impassively at his shoes. Ben hoped that the calmness of his disposition would discourage Chris, proving that he could no longer get under his skin, and drive him away. Ben certainly wouldn't be the first to leave. But Chris didn't step away. He fidgeted a bit, and stared at Ben's distinctive shoes, but he didn't move away from him. Ben even detected, with his heightened perceptual powers, that Chris felt the tiniest bit bad about what he had said.

After a while, Chris asked, "What line of work are you in?"

Ben took this as an olive branch, and allowed himself a

hint of truth. "I'm a software designer," he said.

Chris Schiller brightened at this, and said, "I'm in IT, too."

"I'm not in IT really –"

Chris cut him off. "I like it," he said. "At first the hours were pretty rough. Do you get weekends and holidays off?"

"Not exactly –"

"At first I didn't either. It seemed like one of the bankers always had a problem on Christmas or New Years. Do you get Christmas and New Year's off?"

"No, but –"

"Working on the holidays is tough. Now I run my division, though. Getting there was a real battle. You know how the politics in IT can be."

"I'm not exactly in IT—"

"Now that I'm at the top, things are much better. I only get called in for emergencies during weekends and holidays. It's great. I have time to coach my son's little league team, and my daughter's soccer team. When you have your own family, you'll see how important these things are. That's part of why they love me so much. Don't worry. You'll get your life set up soon enough."

"I don't think so." Ben felt himself becoming increasingly frustrated, which, organically speaking, shouldn't have been possible. He wondered whether something had gone wrong with the pineal implant. It should have been flooding his brain with soothing melatonin.

"Come on, Bentley. You need to have more confidence in yourself."

"I do have—"

"That was always your problem. You're too hard on yourself." Chris slapped him on the back. "Don't worry. You'll get there one day."

Mendel Gerbler be damned, Ben could only abide so much. He had displayed all the modesty he could manage. "I won't get there because I'm already there. I didn't say I was in IT. I said I wrote software. Specifically, I wrote the operating system for communication satellites. There are 1,200 communication satellites operating the Earth, and 1,137 of them run my operating system."

"Well, I never heard of you. I didn't even know communication satellites had operating systems."

"You never heard of me because I don't want you to have heard of me. I run a lab with seven hundred PhDs whose sole job is to think about futuristic technologies."

"You mean like Google."

"Fuck Google! While they're increasing memory for your g-mail account, we're developing an external hard drive that can be implanted in your brain. While they're developing a car that can parallel park, we're building a spaceship that get can get to Mars in three months, and a suspended animation chamber so the astronauts don't age."

"I'm not sure I see the point of going to Mars. It looks like Arizona."

"My scientists have developed an artificial kidney. My

scientists have nearly halted aging. My scientists have developed teleportation. Do you see the point in that? Yesterday, they sent a fork from my laboratory in Silicon Valley to my summer compound in Fire Island."

Chris smiled. "Fire Island, eh? What's the matter, you don't have any forks at your—what did you call it—compound?

"You're a moron, aren't you? It's utterly inconceivable to you that the person you ridiculed as a teenager has been more successful than you. Well, he has. You can call me all the names you want, but that won't change the fact that I could buy you a million times over." Ben had raised his voice to a yell now. This time he lacked the presence of mind to notice that he had come completely undone.

"What do you make?" Ben nearly poked Chris in the chest as he asked this question. "Seventy-five thousand dollars a year? One hundred thousand dollars a year? I make that much in an hour. I came to the reunion by private jet. Not a Gulfstream V or a Cessna or some other shit that you rent from NetJets, I'm talking about a fucking twin-deck, four-engine

Airbus A380. It's bigger than Air Force One. Do you know how much an Airbus A380 costs?"

"I have no idea."

"Of course you don't."

"Three hundred million dollars. And do you know why I don't give a shit how much it costs?"

"Not really."

"Because I get paid one tenth of a cent for every kilobyte of information that gets beamed through those satellite, take a guess what that means I'm worth."

"I don't know. More than 300 million, I suppose."

"I'm worth $32 billion."

"I don't really think material wealth is a measure of success."

"Of course you don't think material wealth is a measure of success, because you have no material wealth. Do you know what the difference is between being a millionaire and a billionaire 32 times over? My home has 27 bedrooms, 29 bathrooms, three kitchens, a lap pool, a basketball court, a bowling alley, and a helicopter landing bay. What do you live in a four-bedroom, three-bathroom splanch in Bethpage?"

"It's a townhouse in Glen Cove. When did you start to bowl?"

"Your children must be ashamed of you."

"My kids love me."

"Your kids don't love you!" Ben was screaming at the top of his lungs now. "You finished 337th in a class of 339 students, and now you're a 44-year old computer technician whose only career aspiration is that he get weekends and holidays off, and who knows less about computers than any random pimple-faced ninth grader at the Bronx High School of Science. Furthermore, lord knows, if the way you treated me is any indication, you probably beat your wife. You're a buffoon and a moron, which makes sense because only a moron could think that his children could love a moron!"

When Ben finished his tirade, he realized that the gymnasium had fallen deathly still. In a soft voice, Chris said,

"Okay, Bentley, take it easy. Sounds like you're a real success. I never meant anything by the names I called you. I was just trying to be funny. It was stupid. I'm gonna let you get back to your compound now."

Then Chris Schiller walked away, leaving Ben standing by himself. Ben looked around the room and felt the eyes of his classmates upon him. They were looking at him, the way they used to, back in high school, the way that haunted him in his nightmares.

There was Stu Koren, by the punchbowl, his mouth agape. There, by the photo retrospective, were Elliot Lent and Nathan Alexander, who'd spent the overwhelming majority of their inseparable nerd childhoods huddled over polyhedral dice and *Renegade Legion* game boards, staring at him as if he were an alien. Briefly, Ben made eye contact with Jill Murray, who looked at him with a measure of pity, which was worse in its own way than the disapprobation of the geeks, until she could not maintain even this, and averted her gaze to the floor.

Breaking the eerie quiet of the gym, Ben heard someone whisper, "Who is that?"

To which came the reply, "I have no idea, but that's the weirdest toupee I have ever seen." Ben considered screaming, "It's not a toupee! It's beaver hair!" But his artificial frontal lobe had kicked in, and he'd begun to assess the situation more objectively. He thought it unlikely that this correction would impress anyone. They almost certainly wouldn't be interested in the superior qualities of beaver mane. Nor, for that matter, would he win any converts by pointing out the other facets of his physical superiority, or remind people of Chris's malicious treatment of him in high school. Ben concluded in his sober judgment that this would seem like ancient history. Ben's oppression at Chris's hands had never exactly been a cause célèbre at Levittown High School, and publicizing it now would seem reactionary to the outburst. Furthermore, Ben's boasts of his own wealth, which had been heard by everyone present, had identified him as a One-Percenter, whereas Chris Schiller universally would be identified as belonging to the fatty meat of the bell curve of Ninety-Nine Percenters. In Ben's view, the impact of this intangible class dynamic could not be overstated and rendered his current deficit in the court of public opinion insurmountable.

So, Ben Brogan turned and left the reunion, silent but for the sound of his $38,000 alligator-skin Testonis clapping against the wooden gym floor. He exited the school through the rear entrance, summoned his limousine, and instructed his driver to get going. He didn't bother to resolve to himself, or observe, that this would be the last time he'd ever set foot in his high school, or the mainland of Long Island, for that matter. This fact was so obvious that it didn't require articulation. He did, however, dial Mendel Gerbler on his cell phone. Gerbler didn't generally take calls in the evening from patients, but Ben had him on a $500,000 per year retainer, which contractually entitled him to weekend and holiday access. He even had a special ring for Ben, and so Ben wasn't surprised when Mendel Gerbler groggily answered the phone by asking, "How did the reunion go?"

"You're fired," Ben replied. Almost instantly, he began to feel better. He'd wanted to fire Gerbler for years. He felt liberated and buoyant. A new therapist might be just the right recipe for happiness. As the Southern State Parkway rolled by, Ben suspected that his improved emotional state could be attributed in part to his artificial pineal gland. Perhaps, finally, it had begun to deliver the melatonin to his system. Melatonin created a virtuous cycle. In his calmer, detached state, he was better in touch with his body, and better able, too, to deconstruct his feelings. In this state of clarity, Ben concluded, just over the border between Massapequa and Amityville, what had gone wrong at the reunion, and what this suggested for the future.

Needless to say, his scientists would have to fix the glitches in the pineal implant. Delaying the delivery of melatonin would not do in the future. But this was tinkering around the edges. It didn't address the root problem. This came to him like an epiphany. The real problem had been his scientists' exclusive focus on the parasympathetic nervous system. In their quest to gain control of the systems that calmed the brain, they'd neglected the systems that agitated it. If they could develop an artificial pituitary implant, and suppress adrenal responses, everything would be different. At the reunion, the failure of his pineal implant wouldn't have mattered; Ben never would have needed it in the first place.

Perhaps it was the melatonin, but as his limousine turned toward off the parkway, near Sayville, Ben felt more optimistic about the future than he had ever been. He would call his scientists first thing in the morning and get them working right away. This was the answer. This was the key to self-mastery. Perhaps, Ben dared to think, if they could get the hormones just right, he wouldn't require a new therapist.

Welcome Back Jataka

In his 549th incarnation, the Buddha returned to Earth as a segmented worm, a fate he accepted with equanimity. The Buddha had had better situations before, but he'd also had worse. More importantly, he'd progressed far enough in his path to Enlightenment not to waste his energy bemoaning a matter outside of his control. After all, how bad did worms really have it? Any fruit fry would give its left wing to live as long and satisfying life as a worm did. Everything died. That was the way of things.

The other worms in his community respected the Buddha greatly. They didn't call him the Buddha, of course. They referred to him by a smell that, in and of itself, didn't greatly distinguish the Buddha. But they had enormous respect for him, nevertheless. Life in the worm world can be frenzied, constantly slithering about, searching for food, making improvements to a burrow, or searching for a new one entirely, fortifying a shelter against flood, dealing with bad digestion, and occasionally hitting the dating scene. There never seemed to be enough time to do everything that needed to get done, let alone to relax, or to think, or to pass an evening with a drink and a friend.

The Buddha, though, didn't seem to be operating by the same clock. He never appeared to be rushed. When he ran into a friend in the loam, he always had time to exchange scents about the day, and, with unfailing politeness, always asked about the other worm's health and family. Most conspicuously, he appeared to be supremely self-possessed, and unburdened by the existential angst that debilitated so many members of their populace. A worm's life is so fleeting! From time to time, a mysterious creature would swoop down from the sky and sweep off with one of their number. Sometimes their fellow worm returned, more often it did not. And worms don't live for very long in the best of circumstances. So, understandably, the worms worried constantly about their futures. What came next? What would their legacy be? Would their burrows be remembered after they had gone? What did it all mean?

To these questions the Buddha offered thoughtful answers. Suffering is everywhere, he said—in birth and death, in sickness and in the struggle for existence. But surely suffering isn't the object of life. Even Gilbert, the most pessimistic of the worms, didn't suppose that an all-powerful worm-God had created the universe solely to make worms suffer. This would create a paradox, for in this story, the worm-God, by causing others to suffer, would become the object of revulsion, and thereby suffer himself. The Buddha had yet to work out many things to his own satisfaction, but he thought it undebatable, as a first principle, that suffering is not intrinsic to existence and could be overcome.

The Buddha suggested that the key to ending suffering was to acknowledge its true cause, the worm mind, and its craving for sensual pleasures, ego gratification and continued existence. If one aspired instead to peace and universal happiness then even the most substantial pains disappeared. For example, a worm named Lydell once scented to the Buddha, "I lifted too much yesterday, and now my pygidium is killing me. Furthermore, I doubt whether it will ever get better, and the attendant anxiety causes me as much or greater pain than the pygidium itself. Have pity on me!" The Buddha responded, "Suffering is always a choice. Some people elect to see illness as an absolute barrier to their happiness. In fact, it is an opportunity. Illness is a natural part of life. If one accepts this premise then it becomes possible to view sickness as an opportunity to connect with our most courageous spirit. Furthermore, not even the most wasting disease can deter our minds from seeking the truth."

Lydell didn't understand. For that matter, few, if any, of the worms understood much of what the Buddha had to say. None of what he taught helped them do anything practical, like find a tasty onion skin or dig a deeper burrow or keep warm on cold nights. But they found the fact that the Buddha had answers to these vexing questions vaguely comforting, and they respected him for the even keel he maintained as well as for his gentle manner with children. Generally speaking, the worm community held him in the highest regard.

For his part, the Buddha didn't think so much of himself. He wasn't self-involved by nature, and he suspected that he had far to go in his quest to master himself. This, and his experience, gave him great modesty. If he'd learned one thing to that point in his lives, it was that the cravings of the ego could never be satisfied, and that indulging these desires led only to suffering. Of course, he didn't refer to this aspect of a worm's personality as the ego. Rather he referenced it by a set of chemicals, which smelled more or less like a mashed turnip. For that matter, the Buddha didn't think of himself as the Buddha. This destiny was in his future. He was merely a worm among worms.

But, at the same time, the Buddha understood that he was different from the other worms. He sensed that he had many lived lives before this one, and would live more to come, and he suspected, further, that he had a gift to share with others before this cycle of death and rebirth would come to an end for him. The Buddha felt that this gift had something to do with the essential quality that differentiated him from the other worms. While they felt eternally stressed and agitated, the Buddha felt jubilant and light. He felt as if he had connected with a higher energy, which freed him from the quotidian concerns that so burdened his friends.

Furthermore, while the other worms experienced the universe solely through their limited sensory powers, the Buddha perceived and felt more. Though he lacked eyes, he could see. Though he lacked ears, he could hear. These abilities, developed through practice, contributed to the Buddha's sense that he had a different, perhaps one might say higher, purpose than the other worms. The Buddha suspected that this design would be revealed in a future life. It perhaps, he thought, might have something do with creatures larger and more complex than his fellow worms.

It would be inaccurate to say that the Buddha gloated in this belief. This would have been surrender to the temptations of ego, to which the Buddha never succumbed. It would be inaccurate, too, to say that the Buddha took joy in his conviction.

The Buddha took joy in every aspect of the universe, in the good soil around him, in his friends, in the diversity of the Earth's flora and fauna. Rather, it would be more accurate to say—it's difficult to find a word that translates the scent well—that the belief *nurtured* the Buddha, in the way that the rain and the sun nurture a forest.

One day, while the Buddha was foraging for dried skin, a creature emerged suddenly from above and lifted him from the soil. With their scents, the other worms cried out, "Oh no, the Buddha is being lifted to his demise!"

"Fear not," the Buddha said calmly, as he rose into the sky. "Death is a natural part of life. Look around you. Trees and flowers and insects die each day, but life continues. We have each lived before and will live again. Do not despair." The other worms thought this was quite a lot to say on the way to one's death, and though the Buddha's presence of mind comforted them, they worried whether they would soon suffer the same fate. On the other hand, the Buddha's subjective experience is best described as elation. He believed that he was taking the next step on his journey, and that his greater purpose would soon be revealed.

If this were so, though, then the Buddha's greater purpose was to be poked and prodded and injected with a substance that made him feel warm and tingly. A man and a woman worked on him. Though he'd never encountered humans before, he sensed that they were an extraordinary species, and that these two were people of science. The Buddha had vague, fond recollections of scientists from his prior lives. Granted, in the insect and reptile community, where he had spent substantial time, science didn't produce much in the way of results. But scientists were always aspirational types, with a strong connection to Nature. Scientists demanded evidence, as opposed to taking things on faith, which the Buddha had found in his experience to be counter-productive and dangerous.

Furthermore, these were kind-hearted people. The man did most of the work, and proceeded gently. Though he was a human and the Buddha a lowly worm, the Buddha could sense the man's concern for his well-being and his wish that the Buddha not experience pain. The woman was equally kind. Sometimes while the man operated, the Buddha wiggled involuntarily. She held him in place with a firm, gentle touch. When the ordeal had ended, she stroked his body, and clucked to him. Though it shouldn't have been possible, this soothed the Buddha. His sensory powers had grown so acute that it he could hear her cooing. In fact, he heard everything.

The woman said to the man. "Do you think this will work?"

"I don't know."

"You are so close."

"One never truly knows when the moment of discovery is nigh."

She nodded.

"If you succeed, what do you think it will mean? What are the ethical implications of immortality?"

"That is a question for the philosophers."

"But surely you have thought about it."

The man smiled, and said, "I have thought only that to live forever with you would be too short, and to live a day without you would be too long." The woman smiled, and kissed the man warmly on the cheek. As she returned the Buddha to the loam, he sensed the great love that she had for the man, and that he had for her in return.

Back home, the Buddha soon sensed that while things and creatures around him had remained the same, he had changed. His friends grew old before his sensory organs, but he seemed immune to the ravages of time. Now, when the worms complained to him about their aches and pains, they inevitably asked, "How do you do it? How do you stay so young?"

"Meditation and a vegetarian diet," the Buddha replied, and he believed this at first. Meditation and vegetarianism can do wonders for one's digestion and general health. But soon he recognized it to be a lie. His friends grew infirm and elderly, and still the Buddha looked like a young worm. Then they began to die, one by one, until only the Buddha remained.

One day, the scientist and his wife extracted the Buddha from the soil. It took more time for them to find him than it usually did. When they found him, they placed him upon a tray, and the woman examined each inch of his body, from his prostomium to his pygidium, with probing touches and gentle caresses.

"My God," she said. "He is entirely unchanged."

"Indeed, this appears to be true," said the man.

"You are a genius."

"My only stroke of genius was marrying you." She kissed him again, and as she returned the Buddha to his home, he sensed that the love between the man and the woman had grown even stronger over the years.

The Buddha missed the company of his friends, but without distractions, he now had more time for his meditations. The Buddha had found that spending quiet time focused on his breath brought him great peace and insight. Now he practiced for hours, sometimes days, on end. He had no sense of time. He sensed only his increasing serenity, his peaceful coexistence with the universe, and his compassion for all living creatures.

From time to time, the scientists extracted the Buddha and chatted with him. They told the Buddha about their children, grant applications, real estate transactions, and all the trivia that friends discuss among one another. Though he treasured his solitude, the Buddha looked forward to these encounters, for he'd come to regard the man and the woman scientist as friends. When the woman began to appear less frequently, the Buddha felt a sense of sadness and then of loss.

One day the man scientist lifted the Buddha up, set him down on the tray, and said, "My wife has died. She has been ill for some time, and now she has died. I tell you this because I feel a closer connection to you than to any other living creature." Then the man sobbed, for how long the Buddha did not know, until finally he cried out in rage, "If I couldn't save her, then what has been the point of all of my work? I've wasted my life!"

Through his meditation, the Buddha had grown sensitive to the ebb and flow of energy in the universe, and he understood the man's ire in this context. The man's love for his wife was a powerful force. Now, having lost its object, it sought another subject to act upon. Finding none, it expressed itself as anger at the man himself. The Buddha felt the man's pain and turmoil and wished that he could do something to help. All he could do, though, was mutter inadequate words of condolence, and say how much the man's wife had mean to him, too. The scientist waved his hand in front of his nose, and gently returned the Buddha to the earth.

There, the Buddha grieved, for he greatly missed the woman, too. He meditated on this. Over time, he came to understand the pain he felt as borne from his desire for permanence, and from his craving of the affirmation that she had given him. The Buddha recognized that these desires, like all sensual desires, could never be satiated. He meditated on this further, until finally the pain of grief had passed, and only the memory of the woman's positive energy remained. This, the Buddha realized, was her essential self.

Through continued meditation, the Buddha gradually

freed himself from all cravings. After a time, he felt no anger toward any creature, and no greed for any worldly possession. He felt neither doubts nor shame. He experienced no restlessness, and felt no torpor. He felt only a sense of perfect peace, a harmony with the universe. Weeks and months and years passed without the Buddha noticing. He no longer felt firmly situated in time. His visits with the scientists grew less frequent, though the Buddha measured this solely by the changes in his friend. The scientist was growing old. His hair had turned to grey, and wrinkles had formed under his eyes. He spoke more slowly than before, and sometimes stumbled while lifting the Buddha from his home or in setting him back.

One day, the scientist said, "My friend, you are going to outlive me. I am dying. It is a struggle for me to get out of bed in the morning. Coming to the laboratory is nearly impossible. I fear that this will be the last time that we will see one another." The scientist paused to catch his breath, and the Buddha sensed now the severity of the illness festering inside the man. He was a kind and strong man, but he wouldn't survive this trial. The Buddha meditated on this briefly and made peace with it.

The man continued, "For a time I thought that my research would succeed in humans. Now I no longer believe this is possible. I haven't even been able to replicate the result in earthworms." He paused again, struggling. "The truth is that I no longer wish to succeed. Since my wife died, so many years ago, life has been an ordeal. I cannot imagine it going on any longer without her."

He smiled. "But you will endure," he said. "You are my great success. You are my contribution to the planet, my legacy. You require no food or water, and yet you do not age." The scientist caressed the Buddha, and said, "I think you are worthy of immortality. You are observant and self-possessed and gentle. I have enjoyed our time together enormously." Then the scientist began to cry, for how long the Buddha did not know. "I will miss you, my friend," he muttered.

When the scientist had finally composed himself, he wiped his eye and said, "You seem like such a wise worm. I wish that you could say something to give him comfort." By this time, the Buddha had grown very wise indeed, but until that moment he hadn't recognized his higher purpose. In that moment, he understood then that he'd placed on the Earth to share his gift with men and women. It was his destiny to show them the road to enlightenment, what he'd come to think of as the One True Path.

So, to the scientist the Buddha said, "Fear not death, my friend, for it is a natural part of life. As a man of science, you know this from experience. Cells within our body die each day, and we live on. When we are cut, we heal and live on too. These are integral parts of the cycle of life. You grieve for your wife, my friend, but your wife lives on even now, as the memories within our minds. We have been changed by our memories of her, and so our interactions with others have been shaped by her. These interactions with creatures large and small change them and in turn create new memories, which alter other future interactions. Through this endless cycle, your wife will live on forever. And so will you. For this is our true, permanent state of existence. Our bodies are ephemeral. We, in the end, are merely energy. This is the key to true knowledge. When one understands this, all apprehension vanishes, for if we are energy then we are eternal, as energy can neither be created nor destroyed." Here the Buddha stretched himself forward, and said, "Do not fear death, my friend, for it is an invitation."

When the Buddha finished delivering these wise words, he felt the deep connection between him and the scientist. They were each on their own journey of discovery, and they had each come so far. How remarkable that fate had brought them together.

In reply, the old scientist pinched his nose. "You have always been a flatulent worm," he said, and then, kind soul that he was, gently placed the Buddha back in his tank and walked away, never to see him again.

Edith Finkelstein's Big Day

That bitch Ethel Schwartz was ruining the most important day of Edith Finkelstein's life. Some people might characterize mistaking the National Women's Project for the National Project for the Woman as a minor thing, but not Edith Finkelstein. She wanted—nay, she demanded—that everything be perfect. This wasn't a dress rehearsal. There would be no second chances. This was the big show, the moment Edith had been dreaming about since she was a child.

Edith could recall thinking about the occasion as far back as the fourth grade. In those days, the restless young Edith primarily worried about superficial matters: what the weather would be like, how many people would attend, what they would wear. Later she became more sophisticated. On Sundays, she often spent entire days at the I.J. Kopelowitz & Sons Funeral Parlor, watching the comings and goings. Kopelowitz's had once been the finest parlor in Brighton Beach, though it had lost a noticeable step by the time Edith began frequenting the establishment. Israel Kopelowitz displayed signs of wear. His abundant nose hair, once contained, had been allowed to grow thick, and Israel Kopelowitz wasn't a handsome man to begin with. He possessed a single black suit, which he deposited at the dry cleaner, religiously, on his way home for Shabbos dinner, and collected on his way to work the following Sunday morning. Thirty years of relentless perchloroethylene treatments had rendered the suit threadbare, in some places translucent, though no one dared tell Kopelowitz, most certainly not Edith. Once when he bent over to pick up a dropped yarmulke, Edith saw the clear outline of his tuchus. But she was a mere child, and Israel Kopelowitz a legend, and a stubborn one at that. His mind had begun to slip. Though he could barely remember the names of his own children, Kopelowitz insisted on continuing to deliver the eulogies himself. In one of his late-career Sunday eulogies, Israel Kopelowitz, seemingly impossibly, misused the word "bereaved." At the service of Keppy Silverman, a door-to-door facial tissue and crayon salesman, he said, "You may be reaved today, but if I have learned one thing in forty years in this business it is that time heals all wounds." Edith couldn't determine conclusively whether the malaprop reflected decline or an underlying lack of intelligence, though Kopelowitz's subsequent sentence, "My prayers go with all of the reft," suggested, at least to Edith, the latter of the two possible inferences.

Even at the tender age of ten, though, Edith recognized that the sorry state of Kopelowitz affairs had as much to do with the deficiencies of the parlor's deceased as the shortcomings of its proprietor. The services weren't memorable because the departed hadn't led memorable lives. Pounding the pavement peddling tissues and crayons was a frivolous enterprise, but no one in Kopelowitz's hallowed halls acknowledged this. To the contrary, one eulogist after another boasted that their parent or spouse or friend subsisted only on Mrs. Stahl's knishes, cursed Walter O'Malley, and had never left Brooklyn, which seemed implausible, but so many people said it that Edith began to believe the truth of this pathetic claim. She sat in the pews and thought to herself, my day will be better than this. It will look better, my friends will be more impressive, and, most importantly, I will have something to show for my life.

Edith confided her aspiration solely to her mother, Ina, who didn't especially approve of Edith's fascination with the death business. Ina generally communicated this through sour faces and muttered "oys" and the other similar tactics to which Jewish mothers customarily resort. Finally, one Sunday evening, in a rare departure from the passive-aggressive paradigm in which she operated most comfortably, Ina confronted her daughter. "Why don't you go outside and play with your friends or do something constructive?" she asked. "There's a kugel-making class starting up at the yeshiva next week. You could take that."

"I want to go to Kopelowitz's," Edith replied, though she liked kugel. "I'm studying for my funeral."

"That's a macabre matter for a ten-year-old to concern herself with."

"But papa always said to be prepared, no?"

Edith's mother couldn't refute that, nor would she if she could. Thinking about her father pained Edith, but to her mother the mere invocation of the subject approached torture. So, that was the end of that. The following Sunday, and each subsequent Sunday for the following decade, Edith returned to the parlor, where her father's spartanly attended funeral had been held, and accumulated data. Even after she left Brighton Beach for the fair shores of Poughkeepsie and Vassar College, she continued to formulate her grand plans, and thereafter dedicated her adulthood to making these dreams a reality.

Now, 74 years after she first set eyes on Israel Kopelowitz, the long-anticipated day had arrived. Each aspect had been planned in exquisite detail, following confabulation with the best and brightest minds in event planning. An aroma therapist told Edith that the scent of lilacs put people at ease, and so she'd ordered 500, enough to supplant the dank must of death with the hopeful bouquet of spring. A shockingly expensive consulting ergonomist helped her identify the finest folding chair, luxuriously plush, and large enough to accommodate even the amplest hindquarters. From her own childhood experience, she knew the risk of mourners nodding off, and so the air conditioning had been turned way up, even though Edith had died two days after the winter solstice. The parlor charged Edith's estate extra for this indulgence, though this expense was minimal in comparison to the cost of the lilacs, out of season, which had to be imported from Brazil, and utterly trivial when measured against the satisfaction Edith derived from the obvious alertness of her guests.

A thousand such flourishes had been attended to, and each gave Edith great pride, though none could compare to her supreme satisfaction in the coffin. This was the sort of detail, the unnoticed nitty-gritty, which distinguishes a truly extraordinary affair from the merely exceptional. Traditional caskets would never have done. Over the years, Edith had laid in and rejected all the traditional favorites. The Canterbury, the Dunstanburgh, the Oxford were solid choices, fine for ordinary folk, but too common for Edith. A 40-year quest led Edith to a pair of

Tasmanian twins, Fanny and Rachael Gillings, who hand-crafted caskets for people with the courage to display individualism, people who—in the Gillings sisters' words—wanted to be "as stylish and imaginative in death as they were in life." *The Mermaid* topped their line. Generously sized and beautifully textured, the pall featured a hand-carved reclining mermaid floating on a richly-hued sea. It was finished with the highest quality brass fittings, a unique hand-felted wool and silk mattress, and a hand-quilted shell-shaped pillow made of 100-percent silk. The brochure touted it the perfect choice for someone with an affinity for the sea. In fact, Edith didn't care for the sea—running water nauseated her—but the aquatic motif created precisely the sort of impression she desired: a self-possessed woman with a love of nature and an appreciation of beauty in all forms.

Edith herself had been done up in style for the big day. It hadn't been easy to arrange for Jeffrey Stein, the finest hairdresser in the city, to do her hair, but after years of persistence, he'd agreed. It cost Edith's estate another $1,000 for the posthumous hairdo, but it had been worth every penny. As she walked by the casket, Sondra Lipschutz whispered to Myra Cohen that Edith looked better dead than alive. Some recently deceased might have taken this the wrong way, but not Edith. A lasting impression of a magnificent coiffure was to her greater glory.

It further pleased Edith to note that each and every one of the bereaved paused, following the payment of their respects, to examine the letters of condolence that had been strategically positioned along the wall opposite the receiving line. Though *The Mermaid* was the quiet star of the show, Edith took every bit as much satisfaction in the admiring responses to the exhibition of letters. Collecting these pieces had been a long and tedious project. Beginning 25 years earlier, she'd written letters under a false name to people she admired—more accurately, to people she thought others admired—telling them of her friend Edith Finkelstein, her contributions to the community, and her recent, unfortunate demise. Edith had been an enormous fan of so-and-so, she would say, and it would mean everything in the world to the Finkelstein family if the famous person would write a few kind words in her behalf.

Some celebrities happily obliged. Art Garfunkel seemed a bit too accessible, frankly. Others required more persistence. Leonard Nimoy responded, after more than six dozen entreaties, with a tired note that missed the point and couldn't be salvaged: "Live long and prosper!" Even the best of the letters needed substantial work. It wouldn't do, of course, to have a letter expressing sadness over Edith Finkelstein's recent death dated decades earlier. Nor would it do for the any of the correspondence to reveal the addressee, Edith's nom de plume, Maria del Toro. Working closely, and under a sworn guarantee of secrecy with John Cotton, the finest framer in the city, Edith redacted the dates and inside addresses of the letters, framing only the letterhead of the notorious person, the substance of the greeting, and the well-known signature.

It had been hard, tedious work, but worth the effort.

Here was a letter from Henry Kissinger recognizing Edith Finkelstein's outstanding humanitarian contributions. Here, a short, predictably sweet and witty message from Jon Stewart: "Now I can hardly wait to go myself." And in the center, her crowning achievement: a handwritten note from J.D. Salinger. "I was saddened to hear of Edith's recent passing," Salinger wrote. "The world was a better place for her love and beauty." The language was perfect. Edith had suggested it to Salinger— approximately 300 times. After he finally succumbed to her persistence, Edith considered, quite seriously, expediting her own demise to ensure that she predeceased Salinger, who according to her intelligence in Cornish, New Hampshire didn't have long left. Losing the letter would have been a colossal waste, but fortunately she went first, praise God.

Such marvelous innuendo! Nothing impressed Arlene Arlen, but she took special note of the Salinger letter. "Did Edith have a Joyce Maynard thing going with J.D.?" Arlene asked Bernice Margaraten, wife of the notorious matzo magnate. Bernice rarely deigned to interact with human beings outside the

Hamptons. She made a point of setting her watch ten minutes slow so she'd never be on time for anything. Yet the Salinger letter captured her attention, too. Seeds of doubt had been planted. "You know," Bernice told Arlene, "I've heard that Edith was a bit of a dish when she was younger." The effect of the letter amazed even Edith.

Everything went precisely according to plan until Ethel Schwartz delivered her eulogy. It was almost impossible to fathom someone confusing the NWP and the NPW. The Women's Project, based in Los Angeles, concentrated on pairing promising women with established mentors, on the theory that aspiring women needed role models. It was touchy-feely, pie in the sky stuff. The Project for Women, Edith Finkelstein's political organization, was grounded in the harsh reality that effecting change required women to hold high political office, which in turn required big money. To this cause, Edith Finkelstein devoted the last 30 years of her life. For the last twelve of these, she'd held the post of development director, which meant she had her hands fully submerged in the dirty, brutish waters of fundraising.

Had Ethel been an ordinary citizen, confusing the groups might have been somewhat understandable, but Ethel was an active member of the NPW, and it was through this activity that she and Edith had become friends. The mistake was utterly incomprehensible given that Edith had her speech written down in front of her. She didn't need to think. She merely needed to read from the cards in front of her, which couldn't have been easier, as each card had been meticulously prepared for the reader's convenience. Edith had printed the cards herself, and mounted each on cardstock to facilitate page turning. She tried out font types and sizes on college speech students to determine the easiest to read, arriving, after substantial testing, on triple-spaced, bold fourteen-point Courier.

Once a month, Edith updated the speeches to include current cultural references and the latest happenings in the non-profit world. Then she printed them out, mounted them on fresh cardstock, and hand delivered them to her attorney, who had strict instructions to review the speeches with each of the eulogists. Indeed, as specified in her will, prior to the service, Edith's lawyer, Hiram Block, had done precisely this. His exhaustive preparation of the eulogists included a review of the pronunciation of difficult words and phrases, such as "esprit de corps," which, despite the advice of counsel, and the phonetic presentation of the phrase in bold fourteen-point print on the cardstock, Ethel mangled into sounding like a military candy. Everything had been done for the convenience of the reader. A monkey could read the speech, but, somehow, Ethel Schwartz could not.

Schwartz continued, "Edith's many innovations as chair of the Social Committee included weekly coffees where all staff members—not just executives—gathered for an open exchange of ideas." From her perch, Edith shook her head. The text clearly reflected Edith's intention that the word "just" be emphasized. The coffees weren't the point of the sentence. Rather, Edith had included this fact to reveal herself as someone who didn't stand on ceremony or judge people by rank or social standing. She was an egalitarian, idea person—a woman of the people. But Ethel Schwartz, by ignoring the carefully placed italics, had fundamentally altered the impact of the passage.

Truth be told, Edith had always harbored reservations about Ethel. She'd been one of Edith's dearest friends, and hence an obvious candidate for the job, but she had an unfortunate tendency to run at the mouth. This proclivity had nearly gotten her kicked out of Sylvia Lakretz's book club when Ethel suggested during a discussion of *The Diving Bell and the Butterfly*—despite Edith's repeated taps under the table—that Bauby had overdramatized things a bit, and how bad was it really to sit at the beach or stare at a tree, never realizing that Lakretz's own father had been locked in. Asked later, Ethel said she interpreted Edith's kicks as a commentary on the macaroons, which, concededly, were dry, and asked why Sylvia ever would have picked the book, given her family history, which was also a fair question. Still, Ethel's poor judgment sounded a warning bell, and who knew whether she could handle the spotlight?

On the other hand, Ethel possessed several substantial assets, which offset her obvious limitations. Principal among these, she contributed to the diversity of the cast. This concern weighed heavily on Edith during the final stages of preparations. Edith very much desired that those speaking on her behalf represent a diverse cross-section of the community. Yet Anna Rosenberg, Sheila Glickstein, and Barbara Berkowitz—each an anchor of the speaker list—all lived on the Upper East Side, as Edith had. Ethel lived on the Upper West Side, lending the ticket balance. This sealed the deal, and during Purim, in the year 5748, Edith Finkelstein asked Ethel Schwartz if she would do her the honor of speaking on her behalf at her funeral.

"Have you died?" Ethel asked, dimly. Edith attributed Ethel's lack of insight to an excess of vodka and hamentaschen, but this would be but the first of many occasions on which Edith would doubt the wisdom of her selection. Once, later, Ethel brought apricot ruggelach to Edith house on bridge night, despite knowing full well that Edith's cat, Fyvush, had a severe allergy to pitted fruits. Edith considered dismissing Ethel, but she lacked the heart, and eventually the notion of Ethel speaking at the funeral gained substantial, irreversible momentum. Now, looking down on the room, Edith regretted that she'd lacked greater courage.

At the podium, Ethel looked up from the notes, which Edith took as another bad sign. Ethel was obviously sizing up the room, although only the pages in front of her required her attention. Ethel had reached the point in the speech dedicated to discussing Edith's gentleness with children. Edith had no particular fondness for kids, but she knew, through experience and extensive focus group testing, that people responded warmly to people who displayed warmth for the young. For the same reason, Edith had included references to her frequent contributions to *The New York Times* Neediest Cases Fund, her annual generous purchase of Samoans despite her allergy to coconut and her status as an organ donor. In a court of law, the ladies and gentlemen of the jury might be less than convinced by these claims, though branding them lies would be inaccurate too.

Most precisely, they reflected confusions of the causal chain. Edith had indeed donated her organs, despite less than robust demand for 80-year-old kidneys, but she'd done so in order that the virtuous act could be referenced in one of her eulogies. So too had she purchased the insipid Girl Scout cookies and displayed occasional kindness to children so that she could incorporate these tidbits into Ethel's panegyric, thereby nurturing the image of her as easygoing and casual.

At this point, Ethel's text said: "Edith Finkelstein possessed a blithe and carefree spirit that was never more evident than in her interactions with children. With five-year-olds she seemed as if she were five years old herself. With teenagers she acted like a teenager. Edith treated children as peers, and they adored her for it. I recall one especially happy occasion when Edith invited the families of the entire sisterhood to her house in Columbia County. My own children still speak of that glorious day. Edith opened her house to us, as she opened her heart to so many others."

Instead, Ethel departed from the prepared remarks and said: "I remember one day, approximately ten years ago, when Edith invited all of the families from the sisterhood up to her castle in the Berkshires. Edith didn't have any children of her own and, in her own way, went about making the place suitable for children: She covered her couches in plastic." People chuckled at this and the favorable reaction inspired Ethel to carry the joke further. "Edith also covered her tables in plastic," Ethel continued. "And her lamps, rugs, and doormats, too. Actually, she covered the entire house in plastic. On your way in and out, you had to zip up." This encouraged further laughter, which, in turn, encouraged Ethel to take the joke further still. "She's the only person I ever met with an autoclave in her kitchen," she said.

The mourners found this uproariously funny. Edith, needless to say, did not. She objected to everything Ethel said. To begin with, grouping Columbia County with the Berkshires was geographically inaccurate and culturally insensitive. More importantly, the shtick about plastic coverings had been dramatically overstated. True, she had covered certain strategic furnishings in plastic, including the couches and rugs, but whom would it have served well if a six-year-old peed on her sectional, as six-year-olds were wont to do? Moreover, Edith had either negligently or maliciously failed to mention that the sectional came from Ethan Allen, and that the doormats, which also had been sealed, were made of mohair. The quality of the furniture made all the difference. And, of course, the house hadn't been covered in plastic. Ethel had presented an exaggerated and one-sided view of things, which did little to bolster Edith's image as easygoing.

The following section of the speech offered an opportunity for redemption. The presentation of Edith's humanitarian work was, in her own view, so powerful that it would undo whatever damage Ethel had caused to that point. Edith waited anxiously for Ethel, who paused for a sip of water. "I would like to continue," Ethel said, "with a story that Edith would have been too modest to share, about her charitable work on behalf of children." Then she paused again. This deeply concerned Edith. Ethel appeared, yet again, to be thinking. Edith positioned her spirit directly in front of Ethel and screamed, "There is no reason to think! Just read!" Instead, at this critical moment, Ethel Schwartz went off the reservation.

"Actually, that's somewhat misleading," she said, and then held up the cards. "You see everything that the other speakers and I are saying is something that Edith herself asked us to say, with the exception of my digression about plastic." As the mourners chuckled, Edith held her face in her hands. "Actually, Edith prepared all of our remarks, word for word. In fact, she prepared every detail of this day."

At this moment, Edith placed her apparition directly in front of her face and screeched, "Shut up, shut up, shut up!" She attempted several haunting tactics, the efficacies of which were uncertain. She tried to curse her, to chill her to the bone, and to excise her immortal soul. When these tactics failed, Edith attempted to strangle Ethel. When this failed too, Edith positioned herself to the side of Hiram Block, her attorney, began poking him in his side and insisted that he obtain an immediate restraining order. When he didn't respond, Edith bellowed with every bit of spiritual energy she could muster, the worst thing she could imagine saying to a lawyer: "I am going to withhold your retainer!" When this also failed to have an effect, Edith sat down next to Kay Margulies, who used to do outreach to the transgender community for Ed Koch, and accepted the debacle.

Sitting among the mourners took Edith back to her days at Kopelowitz's. How surreal to be attending her own funeral! For Edith's taste, the assembly seemed a bit too receptive of Ethel's jokes. Grievers could be nervous. Edith knew this from experience. This made them eager to laugh. But what had Edith done in her life that justified the mutters of "so true, so true," at the claim that she had sheathed her home in plastic? And why weren't they more bothered by Ethel's reliance on the word "actually?" Edith had been careful to eliminate all adverbs from the speeches. Ethel used this one, almost always superfluous, as a crutch.

Ethel continued, "It was Edith's dying wish that we all see her as a free spirit, as a bon vivant, a happy-go-lucky citizen of the world. Actually, everything you have seen and heard today was designed to foster that image—the pictures of her travel, the letters from her impressive admirers, the nice tzedakah box. All of these were part of Edith's concerted effort to construct a certain image. Even these prepared remarks—from which I'm now departing—were written so that you would view Edith as a free spirit. Well, Edith Finkelstein was not a free spirit. She meticulously planned every aspect of her life including, as we see today, most aspects of her death.

"But that's why we loved Edith. It was precisely this attention to detail that made her the woman she was. Edith sent cards for every birthday, anniversary, Bar Mitzvah, death in the family, Rosh Hashanah—you name it, and she corrected the grammar in each and every one of them. She policed popular music for confusion of the subjective and nominative cases and misuse of the subjunctive. If you went to a Bo Diddley concert after the turn of the millennium, you'd have heard him sing

"Whom Do You Love," thanks to Edith's 30-year campaign. Gwen Stefani surely never forgot Edith's furious missive correcting her lyric, "If I was a rich man." And how many quote-unquote "Mens' Rooms'" across the country have benefitted from Edith's roving red pen? Edith left an indelible, unforgettable mark on all of us, and on the world. I only wish that Edith could have seen that we all loved her for who she was, and that I had told her so while there was still time."

Edith sighed. Ethel had a big heart and good intentions, which didn't change the fact that she'd undermined everything Edith had worked toward for her entire life. Ethel had painted a sweet but trite picture of an anal woman without substance. Edith knew from her extensive experience that this portrayal would move some people, but she'd been shooting for more, and anyway, one didn't simply dismiss a lifelong goal in the course of a morning.

The principal success of the conclusion to Ethel's remarks had been to mollify Edith to an emotion state in which she abandoned her plan, conceived at the height of her apoplexy, to haunt Ethel for eternity. Rather, she sat and listened, with all the dispassion she could muster, as the theme of her obsessiveness gathered momentum, like a snowball rolling downhill. First, Anna Rosenberg, emboldened by Ethel, described how Edith stored her canned goods in alphabetical order—as if they could be organized any other way. Then, Barbara Berkowitz elaborated on the extreme measures Edith employed to keep her bathroom germ-free. Finally, Sheila Glickstein earned hearty guffaws for her vivid description of Edith's library of *New Yorkers*, which was arranged chronologically, as if everyone else there just left them lying around their apartments haphazardly.

Edith's agitation and disappointment didn't preclude her from recognizing the goodwill underlying these stories. Each of the speakers seized upon Ethel's theme that Edith attended to her friendships and professional relationships with the same obsessiveness she devoted to her magazines and groceries, and each described, poignantly, how they had benefitted from this attention. It wasn't the image Edith had strived for, but it was less than horrible and, for better or worse, inevitable. In the pews, Edith resigned herself to a legacy as a warm-hearted nagger, and, as Barbara detailed the elaborate measures Edith employed to sterilize her combs and brushes, Edith's thoughts drifted to the future. From her pocket, she extracted a thin brochure, "After Life: The Afterlife and You," with copy every bit as dreadful as the title. The poor quality didn't surprise Edith; she expected such drivel from the goyim.

It did surprise Edith, however, and cause her no small amount of consternation, to learn that her lifelong religious conviction had been incorrect. As she expired, asphyxiated by the bone of a monkfish, Edith thought to herself how cruel irony could be, figured it hadn't been kosher after all, and for this her uppance had come. Shortly thereafter, St. Peter appeared before her, the spitting image of *Match Game* star Gene Rayburn. Peter explained that the New Testament had indeed been the gospel, and that the eternal fates of adherents to other religions depending on an elaborate classification system reflecting the degree to which their own religion differed from Christianity. Edith had been classified "2B." The numeral two referenced a "theistic belief in a deity other than Jesus." The letter B referred to "belief in the God of Abraham and take-away Chinese food."

"Why don't they simply classify me as a Jew?" Edith asked.

"The bureaucracy here is extremely complicated," Peter explained, while holding a preposterously long microphone. "It's better not to ask." Then his assistant, who was the spitting image of Charles Nelson Reilly, handed Edith the pamphlet. "All in all, being 2B isn't so bad," he said. "Buddhists and Hindus have it much worse. The Anglicans have to wait 100 years just to get the pamphlet, all the while waiting in a room that smells like Kings Cross station. You don't want to know what happens to the atheists."

"The pamphlet explains everything," added St. Peter, turning to leave.

"May I ask one question before you go?" Edith said, and

he turned around. "Is it just coincidence or do you bear a striking resemblance to Gene Rayburn?"

"It's no coincidence," he said, gesturing to his assistant. "We have the ability to take on familiar, comfortable forms. Then he smiled, and added, "Who that is, is different for everyone."

As Peter departed, Edith wondered to herself what it meant that the most comfortable figure in her life was the host of a defunct game show. But he was a comfortable figure indeed, whom Edith associated with days off from school and warm tomato soup. How different she would have felt about the hereafter if she'd been greeted by Wink Martindale. Edith had always found him a bit disturbing, and *Tic Tac Dough* had never seemed on the up and up.

She put these matters out of her mind during the funeral, but now, as Barbara Berkowitz prattled on about the challenge of sterilizing a toothbrush, Edith perused the pamphlet. Charles Nelson Reilly had been straight with her. Things didn't seem so bad. Following the funeral, Edith would be obligated to spend an unspecified period of time in purgatory. According to the brochure, purgatory resembled real life. It was hard to get good fruit, and the lines at the motor vehicles bureau were murder. People forgot their death experiences, and so, didn't realize their true whereabouts, although many had a sense of a greater purpose to things. For the most part, purgatory was what you made of it. Luck played a role, but, with exceptions, people got out of it what they put into it, both in terms of effort and their receptiveness to experience. They often formed lasting friendships, and built new families, and, in the end, when someone ascended to a better place, people gathered and felt quite sad. Part of their grief derived from the uncertainty; of course, the bereaved didn't know where their friend or loved one would be going, if anywhere at all. But, mostly, they experienced the sense of loss and uncertainty that accompanies all transitions, and the reflection it encourages on one's own existence.

Reading this, Edith's anger seeped away, and she began to see the opportunity for redemption that the game show hosts had offered her. Edith might not remember everything when she entered purgatory, but she knew herself, and she knew that her essential self would come through. She would retain her goals, her dreams, and her values. She'd still be herself. Given a second chance, Edith knew she could do better. This time around she'd be able to shape people's impression of her in the way she had always dreamed. This time around she would secure more reliable references who would convincingly portray her in the appropriate way. When she ascended, people would come together and celebrate her carefree spirit. This time around, she'd get it right.

The Christmas Miracle Event

Nathan Townsend's father had only ever given him two pieces of advice: One, don't fight a two-front land war in Europe. Two, don't get drunk at the office Christmas party. This wasn't much of a parental legacy, but it seemed like good advice and, up until that evening, he'd faithfully followed both of Herb Townsend's maxims, the first with little or no inconvenience, though the second with some, given Nathan's fondness for eggnog, particularly eggnog with whisky or brandy or rum, each of which were present in abundance at the party, and which, Nathan learned that night, combined to surprising and substantial effect.

Now, the holiday gathering at the Ludwig Andreas Feuerbach School of Ethics and Moral Culture wasn't specifically a Christmas party. That really wouldn't fly with the PTA. Technically, it was a celebration of *Juleaftensdag*, the eve of the pagan winter festival, Yule. The party-planning committee aimed to be broadly inclusive and incorporated elements of many different Germanic heathen cultures. Dried straw was laid across the floor of the gymnasium following the Estonian custom. Each of the first and second graders left a shoe in the window, in the hope they might be visited by one of the thirteen Yule Lads, who imperfectly filled the role of Santa in the Icelandic tradition. Some of the Yule Lads leave modest gifts like potatoes or apples. One helpful fellow, called the Pot-Scraper, cleans the kitchen pans.

The food was similarly multicultural. They had beetroot salad from Finland, roast goose with red cabbage representing Denmark, and sill (pickled herring) from Sweden. The pièce de résistance was a traditional Icelandic food from the Westfjords: fermented skata (stingray) with melted tallow and boiled potatoes. The spread was authentic but grim. Nathan tried the skata and thought it tasted like spoiled bologna. But the liquor was good, and thus Herb Townsend's second adage should have applied, particularly so given that Nathan ate nothing other than the sliver of stingray, and lost count of the glasses of nog.

The trouble began when Nathan got roped into a conversation with Potter Everson. Nathan hated Potter Everson. Potter taught the advanced placement course in history of cynicism and had been voted the senior class's most coveted designation three years running, Least Likely to Inspire. He paraded around the school like a big man on campus, wearing suede moccasins, Madras shorts, and cardigan sweaters, a combination he described as "postmodern hip." At any normal school, the students would have mercilessly teased Potter Everson into an insane asylum, but the students at the Feuerbach school were, by persistent training, tolerant of almost everything (with one notable exception). They embraced Potter Everson. Nathan, however, ordinarily avoided him at all costs.

But thanks to the rum or the brandy or the whisky—he couldn't be sure—Nathan's guard was down, and when Joe Kafka, a grizzled veteran of the science department, grabbed him by the arm and said, "you've got to hear this one," Nathan hardly had time to protest. Before he knew it, he was standing in a large circle which included, among others, Ellen Nordberg, the principal's secretary, Flip Anderson, the custodian who regulated the pool's chlorine content, and Joe Kafka, listening to Potter Everson tell a hilarious story.

"So I'm standing on the corner of 72nd Street and Broadway waiting for the bus, and the Lubavitchers are out in force. The Mitzvah Mobile is parked on the corner and they're scouring the intersection, in full regalia, sloughing off menorahs on unsuspecting pedestrians. They approach the bus line and ask, one person after another, 'Are you Jewish? Are you Jewish?'" Everyone ignores them until they come to this man at the end of the line. He's wearing a derby and a gray raincoat and looking generally meek and vulnerable. 'Are you Jewish?' they ask. He looks at his shoes, and sheepishly says, 'I'm an agnostic.'"

This was met with howls of laughter. In any other environment the story would not have been regarded as especially funny. It probably wouldn't even have qualified as a joke. But at the School of Moral and Ethical Culture, agnostics were regarded with the same derision reserved in the general population for the Polish, hillbillies, and congressmen. As with these comically disfavored minorities, agnostic jokes had become something of an art form—thus the favorable reaction.

Potter went on. "'In that case,' the Lubavitch said, 'You might want to take a menorah—just to be safe.'" Within the circle, chortles and smirks were suppressed, as the faculty and staff eagerly anticipated the punch line.

"So what does the guy in the gray raincoat do?" The group was ready to burst. Wait for it.

"He takes the menorah!"

Hereupon followed howls of laughter, shortness of breath, and general glee. Ellen Nordberg grabbed her stomach to keep from keeling over. Flip Anderson wiped tears from his eyes. Doris Keeling, the third-grade teacher, suffered a paroxysm. The wave of euphoria infected everyone, except for Nathan, who didn't find the story amusing at all. To the contrary, he found it decidedly annoying.

In retrospect, Nathan would find it difficult to explain why he had such a negative reaction to the joke. He'd heard agnostics made fun of many times. While, for a variety of reasons, he didn't find the jokes particularly funny, he didn't regard them as offensive, since religion, unlike race or ethnicity, was a matter of personal choice. Thus, within the precise ethical code of the school, the subject was fair game. But he had a negative reaction all the same. Whereas everyone else was in hysterics, Nathan groused and frowned and moped. Then, without thinking, he muttered, "I'm an agnostic."

Ellen Nordberg spit out her raspberry seltzer. She thought it was part of the joke.

Joe Kafka hit him on the back and said, "That's a good one, Nate."

But Nathan said, "No, I'm serious," with a look that showed he really was. "I'm an agnostic," he repeated.

The room rapidly deflated. Nathan Townsend was both lucky and unlucky in this moment. At another school, they wouldn't have cared that he was an agnostic. So that was unlucky. But at another school where agnostics were scorned, they might have openly derided him. On this count Nate was lucky. In the rigorously precise ethic of the Feuerbach School, it was decidedly unacceptable to mock someone to their face, no matter what the offense. Thus no one dared ridicule Nathan openly.

But Nathan might more popularly have admitted that he had leprosy. At the Feuerbach School, it went without saying that everyone was expected to be an atheist or, more precisely, a secular humanist. Secular humanism is a value system that embraces reason and justice and rejects religion as a basis for moral decision-making. This repudiation of dogma was utterly essential to the culture of the school. The following quotation was emblazoned above the main door, through which each student and faculty member walked every day:

"RELIGION IS ALL BUNK"

Thomas Alva Edison

So fervently committed to this outlook on life was the

leadership of the Feuerbach School that it had been trying for years to have the American government recognize secular humanism as a religion. To the indoctrinated observer, this might appear to be a contradiction, but to the Feuerbach school it was a matter of high principle. Also, the designation carried with it certain tax advantages. Inevitably, the debate had devolved into litigation, which wasn't going well for the school. The trial judge, and the members of a unanimous appellate court panel, had all attached great weight to the Edison quote. In the view of the school's attorneys, this was too literal a reading of the quote above the door. For example, the following colloquy occurred during the argument before the Second Circuit Court of Appeals sitting *en banc*:

JUDGE HIRAM FERNANDEZ: Counsel, how can you argue that the Feuerbach School has a religious mission, and hence entitled to IRS Code Section 501(c)(3) status when the sign above your door says,

"Religion is all bunk?"

WILLIAM DALEY, ESQ. (of Daley, Daley, Daley & Dealey): Your Honors, with all due respect, I submit you are reading the inscription too literally.

JUDGE HIRAM FERNANDEZ: Oh. How should I read it?

WILLIAM DALEY, ESQ.: The critical point is that my clients are zealously dedicated to their absence of faith-based conviction. One might reasonably say that they are…religious about it.

JUDGE HIRAM FERNANDEZ: I see. Very clever.

In truth, Hiram Fernandez was not impressed at all and, as every lawyer knows, so goes Hiram Fernandez, so goes the Second Circuit. The school lost the appeal 9-0. Bill Daley blustered to the press about an appeal to the Supreme Court, but no one at Feuerbach held out much hope, and the case was something of a sore spot at the school.

So, it went without saying, that atheism (or secular

humanism) was expected among the staff.

"Don't you believe in the scientific method?" Joe Kafka asked, incredulously.

"I certainly believe in the fact of it," Nathan said. "And I believe it has produced many socially useful results."

"Then why are you willing to make a leap of faith and say that God may exist?"

"Let me ask *you* this," Nathan replied. "Applying scientific evidence, what evidence is there that God does not exist?

"Only my experience," Joe said.

"Is it not then a leap of faith to say that he does not exist?"

Joe Kafka had no answer. Silently, he took a step away from Nathan. So too did Potter Everson and Ellen Nordberg. Even Doris Keeling retreated, and she could tolerate almost anything. Her husband had been having an open affair with a goat for 30 years. One by one, the faculty and staff filtered away until only Flip Anderson remained.

Quietly, Nathan asked, "Flip, do you really believe there's no chance that God exists?"

"Well, he sure don't keep the chlorine levels straight," Flip replied. Then he walked away, leaving Nathan alone.

*

At Hi Life, on 83rd and Amsterdam, Nathan related the story to his friend, Lou Pinto, an Eastern Grey Kangaroo who Nathan had met several years earlier at a Bikram yoga class. Nathan didn't stick with it—the moist heat aggravated his sinuses—but Lou had, which was ironic in a way, because he had a bit of a temper and, generally speaking, didn't seem the Yogic type. Nevertheless, he was now enviably flexible.

Lou lived all the way on the East Side, but he was always happy to go out for a drink. He didn't sleep much, and besides, it was Christmas Eve. Indeed, the Hi Life patrons were dudded up in festive reds and greens with floppy Santa Claus hats hanging from their heads, drinks in their hands, and cheeks aglow. The room was abuzz, abounded in good holiday cheer, which had affected everyone, everyone that is except for Nathan Townsend. Lou Pinto noticed as soon as he hopped in.

"Who died?" he asked. "You look like someone killed Santa Claus."

Nathan told him what happened.

"That's too bad," Lou said with obvious sincerity. Lou was a good and patient listener. "Why do you think you said it?" he asked. "Was it the nog?"

"Maybe," Nathan said, "But I really think it was that Potter Everson. Something about him always throws me off."

Lou nodded. "What do you think is going to happen to you?"

"Nothing, I suppose."

"You have tenure, after all."

"True."

"So why are you beating yourself up about it?"

Nathan sighed. "I'm jealous," he said. "I look at my colleagues at the school with envy. They have conviction about things, about what's right and wrong, and the ultimate direction and meaning of life. It gives them a sense of purpose and certainty. Perhaps it's smug on their part. I don't know. Call it what you will, but it seems like a happier life they have."

"You can have that life too," Lou said.

Nathan's face revealed his inner turmoil. "It isn't as easy as that," he said.

"Why not, brother?"

"I have doubts! I have such doubts!" Nathan said. "I look around me and everything I see fills me with awe. Soaring birds, glorious plants, fish of every size, shape, and color. Mountains which touch the sky and volcanoes miles under the sea. Animals of every size, shape and color imaginable. Such wondrous life! Could it truly be all random? Perhaps, but can anyone be sure?" He looked up from his drink and faced Lou. "Don't you ever have doubt?"

This was a bad question. Lou's father had been grossly

abusive. If he failed to clean his room or talked out of turn, his father would box him, often in public. Years of therapy and tantric meditation had helped Lou release the anger, but he had no uncertainty about the absence of God.

"No," Lou said.

"How can it be that easy for you?"

"It's just a matter of faith," Lou said.

Nathan nodded. "If only I could make the leap," he said.

Lou smiled. "We've both probably had enough to drink," he said. "How about I walk you home?"

"It's all the way on the east side, completely out of your way."

"What are friends for?"

Lou was a good one. He even pulled his wallet from his pouch and picked up the tab.

*

The Central Park Reservoir can be spectacular on a winter evening. In the cold crisp air, the lights of the New York skyline reflect off the water. It's a sight without parallel in the great cities of the world, and that evening was as fine as any there had ever been. Lou Pinto appreciated its beauty. He'd jogged around this track countless times, often late at night, but he had never seen anything like this. He hoped the nighttime splendor would cheer Nathan, but it had no effect. His friend stared at the ground as he trudged along, moping.

Lou felt his friend's pain. He didn't specifically understand the angst of a crisis of faith. Lou had never questioned the nonexistence of God. For him this had always been axiomatic. But he knew what it was like to be different from those around you, to be an outsider. This anguish he understood all too well. He placed a gentle arm around the shoulder of his friend, and tried to absorb some of the hurt. Sadly, it had no effect.

As they neared the Southeast Gatehouse, a fog began to roll in. At first it didn't seem unusual, other than the fact of it on such a luminous night, but it progressed with preternatural dispatch and had to it an otherworldly density and odor. In the course of no more than twenty steps, Nathan and Lou had moved from crystal clear Christmas air to a dense, miasmic thicket. Instinctively, they turned to retrace their steps, but the brume had closed in on them from behind too and, presently, there was no escape. They took a few clumsy steps forward or, more accurately, in the direction they believed to be forward. But Lou, normally sure of foot, stumbled, and then they stopped in their tracks.

Just as he spoke, an ill wind blew through. It sent a chill up Nathan's spine and activated the dull ache in Lou's trick knee, which he'd injured twenty years earlier running the Tel Aviv Marathon. Lou sensed trouble afoot. The joint only bothered him when something bad was about to happen. The last time it hurt him, he got home from work to find that a wallaby he was dating had absconded with his collection of *Howard the Duck* comic books.

When the gust died down, the air immediately before them had cleared a bit, just enough so that Nathan and Lou could see standing before them the apparition of a figure from the past. With his mutton chops, long coat and vest, he could have been any nineteenth century English gentleman out for a postprandial constitutional. But he was unmistakably the famous English biologist—staunch advocate of Darwin, notorious verbal sparring partner of Samuel Wilberforce, and coiner of the term "agnostic." His name rolled gently off of Nathan and Lou's tongues.

"Thomas Henry Huxley," they said softly, in unison.

"Which of you is Nathan Townsend?" the specter asked.

"Who wants to know?" Lou asked protectively. It seemed odd that this apparently supernatural creature didn't know whether Nathan was a human being or a kangaroo.

"I have been sent with an important message for Nathan Townsend."

"How do we know you're authentic?" Lou repeated. The ghost's voice had the appropriate resonance and vibrato, but Lou wanted hard proof.

"When he was seven years old he had to have an impacted marble surgically removed from his right nostril."

"Anyone could know that. It's a public record."

"It was specifically, a blue marble from the game *Mouse Trap*. He was frustrated because the swinging boot never functioned properly."

Lou looked at Nathan.

"It's true," Nathan said. "He's for real."

Lou looked back at the phantasm. "What is it then? What do you have to say?"

"I have been told to tell you this conclusively once and for all." Here, the ghost of Thomas Henry Huxley paused for dramatic effect. "There is no God!" The proclamation resonated through the red maples and pin oaks of the nearby Ramble. In the distance, an owl hooted.

"How do you know this?" Nathan asked.

"I have been told so by an omniscient, all-knowing being

whose credibility I can personally verify."

"Then that would be God," said Lou.

"No," said Huxley. "He sees and knows all, but his power has limits."

"Such as?"

"He is very poor at golf. He has taken lessons for thousands of years but he still slices. He also has great difficulty getting the chlorine right in his hot tub."

"I've heard that can be difficult," Nathan said.

"He knows of your anguish, Nathan Townsend. He wants your mind to be at ease."

"Thank you," said Nathan.

Huxley turned. "And Lou Pinto, he told me to tell you that your father loved you very much."

Tears formed in Lou's eyes. It was the greatest gift anyone could have given him. "Thank you," he said. "Thank you so much."

But Thomas Henry Huxley was already gone.

*

When the fog lifted, Nathan felt as if an enormous weight had also been lifted from his own shoulders. It didn't seem it should be so easy to secure peace of mind, but Huxley had given it to him. Now he had certainty and conviction, and this in turn made him buoyant. Nathan resumed their walk home with a spring in his step, and an unfamiliar sense of optimism.

"You look like a new man," Lou said, who felt a great sense of relief himself. "It's a Christmas miracle."

Nathan corrected him. "A miracle event," he said. "A Christmas miracle event."

Lou smiled, and together they walked into the holiday night.

Made in United States
North Haven, CT
29 October 2022

26076028R00136